SILENT ROSE

Paisley Jacobs

WHISPERS OF VICE AND VIRTUE TRILOGY

This is a work of fiction. Names, characters, places, and incidents are products of the author's imagination are used fictitiously, and are not to be constructed as real. Any resemblance to actual events, locales, organizations, or persons living or dead, is entirely coincidental.

ISBN: 9798218677336

To Catherine,

You believed in me at times when I didn't believe in myself. If I fell, you picked me back up. I will always remember your kindness. Thank you for being my most devoted supporter

CONTENT WARNINGS

Katoptronophilia

Edging

Temperature play

Torture

Childhood trauma & neglect

Violence & Murder

Drug/Alcohol use

PTSD nightmares

PLAYLIST

Iris - The Goo Goo Dolls

Dirty Little Secret - Nessa Barrett

Love the Way You Hate Me - Like A Storm

Nightcrawler - Travis Scott, Swae Lee, Chief Keef

Bad Reputation - Joan Jett & the Blackhearts

Secrets and Lies - Ruelle

J's Lullaby - Delaney Bailey

Disturbia - Rihanna

Criminal - Britney Spears

Love Is Madness - Thirty Seconds To Mars, Halsey

Crave - Tove Lo

LoveGame - Lady Gaga

Die For You - The Weeknd

Let's Get Lost - G-Eazy, Devon Baldwin

Psycho - Mia Rodriguez

Good Girls Go Bad - Cobra Starship, Leighton Meester

Slow Down - Chase Atlantic

Can You Hold Me - NF, Britt Nicole

I Hate You, I Love You - Gnash, Olivia O'Brien

Trauma - NF

For anyone who has ever lost themselves in trauma. You're not alone, and you will make it out stronger than ever.

CHAPTER 1

Rosanna

Stealthy, deadly, and curious. It's what I have to be as a mafia spy: listening to whispers that could get me killed, and risking exposure as the daughter of a Mariano. I would love for people to know who I am, but unfortunately, that is not my reality. I have a reputation to uphold after all.

I enjoy nights when I get to eavesdrop on powerful men, expose their secrets, use them as blackmail, or, in some cases, bring justice to those who were wronged.

Nicolai's club, La Citta del Peccato, is the perfect place to spy without getting caught. It's dark, and most people are too intoxicated to pay attention to the real reason I'm here. Also, Gia and Angelina enjoy partying at this club, so they tag along. With them at my side, I don't look suspicious showing up by myself, or if I get into any trouble, they'll back me up.

We get to the club around one a.m. It's peak partying hour, so everyone is dancing, drunk, and far too distracted to pay attention to anything but themselves. Dressed in a tight black spaghetti strap dress with a square neckline and my favorite go-to combat boots, paired with my long, straightened, inky hair and a passable smoky eye, I look like a badass bombshell, and I'll blend into the shadows.

Gia and Angelina are ordering drinks at the bar with Nicolai right behind them, scanning the club for any threats. He does that constantly after what happened, and I don't blame him. If anything, I'm grateful that he is protecting my friends.

Sticking to the shadows, I avoid too-interested men eager to buy a pretty woman a drink. As much as I appreciate the attention, it gets annoying. I'm on a mission, not on the pursuit of a one-night stand, no matter how tempting that thought is.

Squeezing through the crowd, I keep my head down and my footsteps light as I approach the stairs of the VIP room. After making subtle eye contact with the security guard, he lets me pass. As Nicolai's wife's best friend, I am on the list for VIP access. But I don't go in. Instead, I tiptoe up the stairs until I'm within earshot of the room, nonchalantly lean against the wall, and pull out my phone to scroll on social media.

I've learned the routine of the VIP regulars, most of whom are wife-cheaters or wife-beaters. The rest are fuckboys, gamblers in debt, and one guy in particular kidnapped my best friend. Fuck that guy.

Around this time, they're invested in poker rounds for at least two more hours. It's rare for them to exit the room, but if they do, I can play it off or sneak away. Why would they have to leave anyway? They have access to a fully stocked bar, bathroom, and enough cigars to last a lifetime.

The sound of them laying out their poker plays is audible through the wall, and one man shouts that he won with a full house.

Carlo D'Amico's distinct voice says, "Damnit. I was gonna buy a new boat with that cash."

"Oh, cry about it. You already have a boat," someone jabs.

"Yeah, but I need a bigger one for all the ladies I'm gonna load it with." Carlo has plenty of money to buy another fancy toy; he just likes to gloat about his riches after losing the game.

"I'm sure your wife would love that." Now that voice sounds familiar. Rocco Accardi.

I peek around the corner to see the older man glaring at Rocco, who just grins tauntingly.

"Are you two done bickering like babies so we can play another game? Or would you rather pull your dicks out and measure who's longer?"

Luca Moschelli—Italy's biggest fuck boy. He's 36 years old, works for his daddy, and is known as a total douchebag.

Rocco nods toward the game, indicating for the dealer to deal him in. Everyone adds a wad of cash to the stack, and by the time the table's all in, there's enough money in the middle to buy a car.

Luca wins the next round with a lucky royal flush and Carlo is pissed but doesn't do anything about it. He's too old to take any of the other men on.

Aimone Moschelli walks up the stairs, eyeing me as he passes. On the rare occasion that men have walked by me in the darkened hallway, they always assume I'm a hooker waiting on one of the guys. They underestimate me, and that's their downfall.

As soon as Aimone enters the VIP room, Luca, his older brother, protests. Apparently, he's had to clean up a few of his sibling's mistakes in the past. As to what those "mistakes" are, I'm still looking into that.

"The fuck are you doing here?" Oh, Luca is pissed.

"Playing poker. Why else would I be here?" Aimone asks.

"You're only 23. You don't even know how to play poker."

"Wanna bet?" Aimone challenges.

Luca crosses his arms. "Fine. If you win a game with me, you can have Caterina. If I win, you go home and never step foot in this club again."

"Deal."

Typical men, gambling women as if they're property. If a man ever does that to me, I will personally cut his balls off and force-feed them to him.

The dealer passes cards to both Moschelli men, but it's too far away for me to see what hand they're going to play, so I hide against the wall and listen. No one speaks; the audience is either too focused or too scared to speak up during the game.

I peek around the corner again. Grinning, Luca is the first to lay his cards down. "Full house."

Aimone tilts his head back. "Aw, fuck." He lays his hand down with a smile full of mischief. "Four of a kind. Caterina's mine."

Luca's face turns pale as he signals to talk with his brother away from the others. The pair moves to the corner of the VIP room, right where I can see them without being caught.

"A deal is a deal. Suck it up, big bro," Aimone says.

"Of course, you know I'm not the type to break my word. I just need to clarify. Is this going to be like last time? I don't want to clean up your mess again, Aimone. I mean it."

"Not my fault she couldn't keep her mouth shut!" It seems like Aimone has anger issues.

"Yeah, well, it is your fault she was blabbing around in the first place. Or is it her fault too that you couldn't ask for consent and keep your dick in your pants?"

Bingo.

Aimone jams his finger into Luca's chest. "Watch your mouth. We will finish this discussion at home."

Luca puts on a fake smile. "Just making sure we're on the same page, lil bro."

His brother nods in understanding.

My skin prickles, and I look away from the Moschelli brothers and meet the gaze of dark eyes. *Shit.* They're partially hidden beneath his wavy, black locks of hair, but I can tell they're dead set on me. Rocco grins. How long has he been watching me? What's he going to do about it? I break eye contact and start to run down the stairs until a pair of tatted, muscular arms trap my body against the wall.

"Can I help you with something?"

Rocco tilts his head, studying me. "What were you doing up there?"

I scoff, acting unaffected. "Not that it's any of your business, but I was waiting for someone."

"Really?" Clearly, he doesn't believe me. "Who may that be?"

"Aimone."

He laughs, and the sound is beautiful. I hate it. "Aimone Moschelli?"

"Yep. Now, if you'll excuse me." I try to sneak out from under his arms, but he stops me with a hand on my wrist.

"I'm feeling generous. How about I help? Come with me."

Damnit.

Yanking my wrist out of his grasp, I growl, "The last thing I need is help from you."

"Feisty. I like it. You said you were waiting on Aimone. I'll take you to him… Unless that's not what you were doing up here?" He stares at me, stubbornly waiting for an answer.

He pauses. "Unless that's not what you were doing up there?"

He stares at me, waiting for an answer. I have to force the words out of me.

"No, I would appreciate the help. Thank you." Let's hope I can get away with this lie, or else I'm fucked.

I walk back up the stairs with Rocco's hand on my lower back, as if I might fall. I shove him off, but that only makes him grin again. I'm getting tired of his cockiness.

When I stand in front of Aimone, his eyes move down my body. It makes my skin crawl.

"Rosanna here claims she was waiting for you. It's not polite to leave a lady in waiting, so I brought her to you. Is this true?"

How does he know my name?

I don't want to, but I play the part of a hooker. I smile, bat my eyelashes, and put my arms around his neck as I sit on his lap.

"Thank you, Rocco, you can leave now," Aimone says without taking his eyes off me.

I seriously cannot stand his hands on my thighs and hips. It disgusts me. He's not my type—too young, perfect-looking, and fake like a Ken doll. Never mind the fact he may be a rapist.

Rocco walks away and takes a seat at the poker table across from us. His stare never wavers, but I pretend not to notice.

Aimone drags his nose up my neck. "Who sent you? I must thank them. This is the best gift I've ever received. You are smoking."

I hate this. I put my finger to his lips. "Shh. It's a secret, baby. How about you enjoy the gift rather than question it?"

"Alright, I'm out of here. No way am I watching my lil bro go at it. Have fun but not too much fun," Luca comments with a hint of threat in his tone.

Aimone hums a "Mmm" while kissing my neck. Tilting my head to give him better access, I glance over at Rocco, and his stare has changed from amusing to… is that jealousy? He's gripping the table so tightly that his knuckles are white.

With a smug grin, I fiddle with Aimone's shirt and whisper in his ear, "Can we go somewhere more private? So you can get your money's worth."

"You read my mind." As he shifts to get up, I feel his erection against my ass and I almost gag.

Rocco's glare never falters on us as we leave the room hand in hand. As soon as we're downstairs, I survey the club and wink at Angelina and Gia—our signal that the fun is about to begin.

Pulling my new mark along, I head to the club's basement. "I know somewhere we can be alone. Follow me."

"I've never been down here. How'd you get access?"

"The owner and I are closely acquainted," I state, purposefully making it sound like I'm sleeping with the owner even though I most definitely am not.

After we step through the door, I subtly leave it cracked open so Angelina and Gia can enter.

As I push Aimone onto a chair, he purrs, "Damn. I'm not usually into submissive, but you're so hot I can't complain."

I sit on his lap, tightening my thighs around his hips so he can't get up. "Get used to it, baby. We've just started."

Tilting forward, I distract Aimone with a full view of my tits as I zip tie his hands behind his back, and then I drop to my knees to do the same with his feet.

"I have to say this is a first for me. I'm typically the one doing the tying if you know what I mean," he laughs.

Disgusting.

I stand back to admire my work and kiss his cheek. "Wait here. I have a surprise for you. I just have to change first."

"Oh, hell yeah. Can't wait."

In the attached bathroom, where my extra clothes are, I get ready for our "fun" by throwing my hair up into a ponytail and dressing in black cargo pants and a tank top—my "work uniform." The final touch—black lipstick. My best friends join me to change into their alternative outfits. A jumpsuit, black high-top boots, and red lipstick for Angelina. And a black skirt, sleeveless top, thigh-high boots, and pink lipstick for Gia. The different colors are our signatures.

"Who is he and what'd he do?" Angelina asks as she slides gloves onto her hands.

"Aimone Moschelli. I'm not sure yet. I just heard he has an ugly past. My gut is warning me about this one. I was gonna wait for more information to pounce, but I kind of got into a predicament I couldn't get out of."

"Guess we will have to find out."

"Oooh, it's kind of like the game Clue!" Gia exclaims. "This is gonna be so much fun!"

As we walk out, Aimone's eyes light up. "Oh shit. Three of you? It can't get any better than this." When my bestie gets closer, a look of confusion takes over his excited expression. "Wait. Angelina Vittori? You're Nicolai's wife."

The club owner's voice cuts in, "She sure is. Touch her, and I will kill you myself. But don't worry, they'll do that for me."

Aimone looks at all of us, obviously trying to figure out what's going on.

"Have fun, ladies. Aimone, it was nice knowing you, but truthfully, it wasn't." Nico kisses Angelina, hands her a folder, and walks out, leaving us to our fun.

My friend opens the file, and it's exactly what I expected—a picture of a young girl covered in bite marks, bruises, a bruised neck, blood and cum on her thighs, and even bald spots on her scalp. She was brutally raped by Aimone Moschelli, and he got away with it. The girl killed herself the following day.

"What the fuck is going on here?!" The man of the hour shouts.

Angelina holds up the photo, and his face pales. "We're going to have so much fun with you."

"I have no idea who that is." Such a blatant lie.

"Is that because she is barely recognizable after what you did, or are you just a liar? Because you're not a very good one at that," I deadpan.

This is how girl nights typically go— Angelina does the torturing, I do the talking and control the mind games, and Gia cleans up the mess at the end.

I stare at our victim's scared, helpless expression as Angelina saunters behind him to lay her hands on his shoulders.

"Do you enjoy biting younger girls?" I inquire. "She was covered in marks. They would have scarred if she had survived, but she couldn't live with what you did to her."

"She liked it. She screamed for me!"

My friend's nails sink deep into his skin, making him scream. The resulting wound looks almost like a bite mark.

"Poor baby. Wrong answer. Try again."

He seethes, "Yes. I enjoyed every second of it."

"I think Aimone's zip ties are a little loose. Angelina, would you mind tightening those for me?"

She pulls on the zip ties so hard they dig into his skin.

"Ow! What do you want? Let me go, and my father will give you enough money for all three of you to survive on."

"Look at you. Such a daddy's boy. It's pathetic, you know? Relying on his money to cover up your fuck ups. Did you rape her to feel powerful? Did you go home and brag to dear old daddy?"

His expression is full of rage as he tries to avoid my gaze, so I grab his jaw and force him to look back at me. "Answer me."

"Yes."

"And was he proud?"

No answer. I nod at Angelina, and she slaps him across the face.

"Was he proud?!"

Aimone can't meet my eyes. "No."

"That's right. Just because you took advantage of a little girl doesn't make you a powerful man. I bet your daddy hated you after you told him. I bet he wished you were never born." I lean in and whisper, "You're a fucking coward."

He starts to cry. It's quite pathetic how quickly we broke him. "What do you want?"

"We want you to acknowledge your actions, and we want justice for her."

Angelina slices a knife across his thigh.

"Okay, okay. I'm sorry! I'm so sorry for hurting her. Please let me go," he sobs.

"Hmm. Apology not accepted. Your actions cost someone their life, and now we're going to take yours."

"My father and brother will kill you if you murder me."

That makes the girls and me giggle. "They can try."

An hour passes, and Aimone is barely alive. He's crying like a baby; he pissed his pants and has vomited all over his clothes.

I lift his droopy head to make him meet my eyes. "You will never hurt a girl again. Men like you shouldn't get to walk away like nothing happened. That girl killed herself because of how badly you traumatized her. We can't just let you go after that. I'm sure you understand."

I walk out of the splash zone before Angelina slits his throat.

"C'mon. I have to clean all that up, you know," Gia grumbles.

"I'll help," Angelina groans.

"No, no, no. I can't risk your fingerprints, and you'd probably make it harder to clean up than it needs to be. You girls go home. I'll handle this."

Gia gets slightly grossed out by the torture and murder, so she distracts herself from the scene by messing around on her phone. However, when it comes to the aftermath, she falls into a whole different mental state. My friend has always been a clean freak, so she tends to enjoy cleaning up our mess. Plus, she does a really good job at it. By the time she's done, it'll be like we never brought someone down here in the first place.

Lipsticks in hand, we surround Aimone's lifeless body, and I tear his shirt off to wipe his bloody face. On his forehead, I write "Rapist" in black. Angelina writes "Predator" on his right cheek in red, and on the other cheek, Gia writes "Killer" in pink.

It's our tradition, our calling card. Everyone will know what Aimone did and that they're next if they do the same. We want it that way. We want people to be scared of us. You don't fuck with the Whispers of Vice and Virtue.

CHAPTER 2

Rocco

The last person I expected to show up tonight was Rosanna Mariano, the bane of my existence. Even though I've only met her twice, she has made me weak, obsessed, distracted, and a madman. What is it about her that has me so hooked? Since that night she walked through the club, I haven't been able to forget about her. It doesn't help that she murdered Angelina's father in cold blood, and I had a front-row seat to it. God, that was the hottest thing I have witnessed in all of my 28 years.

Is it how she always keeps me guessing? Am I just attracted to her and need to get laid? Or do I want to corrupt a perfect, pristine little Mariano? I can't figure it out, and it's driving me insane.

When she gets up to leave the VIP room with Aimone, my thoughts whirl. *Don't follow them. Let it go, Rocco. Yeah, fuck that.*

I rise from my chair abruptly, and everyone looks toward me at my rude interruption, but I don't owe them an explanation. I rush down the stairs to look for my obsession, but it's ridiculously packed. In my hurry, I run into a girl and almost knock her over. Shit, that was rude of me. I help her up and apologize quickly, but when she tries to flirt, I run away before she can finish her proposition. I'm not interested.

I've officially gone mad. An hour has passed, and I'm running around the club like a lost boy in a grocery store. I can't even locate Angelina to ask where her friend went. Hell, I don't even know what I'll say when I find Rosanna. Maybe I won't say anything, I'll just punch that smug look off Aimone's face.

Time for plan B—insurance that she won't leave with that bastard tonight.

I head outside and lean down to pretend to tie my shoe next to Rosanna's black Challenger. With a small flick of my pocketknife, I puncture her back tire. Aimone's car is next— his license plate simply reads "Aimone." Show off. I slash all of his tires for the fun of it. She's going nowhere with him. I move my dark blue and black bike to the parking spot next to the Challenger and wait, but she doesn't come outside for another thirty minutes.

What the fuck were they doing for an hour and a half?

Rosanna doesn't notice me with my helmet on, so I get to witness her reaction to the flat tire. "You've got to be kidding me."

I pull my helmet off. "Something wrong?"

"Even better. You're here," she grumbles sarcastically. "I have a flat tire. I must've run over a nail or something."

"Hop on."

The woman looks at me like I'm crazy. "Excuse me?"

I extend my helmet to her. "I only have one, but I don't need it."

"You want me to get on that death trap?"

"I would never hurt you."

"Says the man who literally kidnapped my best friend!"

"Well, sweetheart, it looks like you don't have much of a choice. Walk home, or ride me." *Shit.* "Ride with me, I mean."

She raises an eyebrow. "If I accept this favor, you know I don't forgive you and still hate you, right?"

"Of course." I'd rather her hate me than not know me at all.

Rosanna tries to take the helmet from my hands, but I pull it back. The thing is way too big for her head, so I'll be putting it on her to ensure it's going to stay on for the ride.

"Let me."

She crosses her arms, and the move pushes her tits up. It takes everything in me not to look down, but I'm not a douchebag so my eyes remain on her face.

I pull the helmet over her head, tighten the straps, and shake it. It's as secure as it'll get. I hop on the bike and nod for her to settle in behind me. Rosanna has to hike her dress up to sit down. *Lord, help me.*

The bike roars to life. I love the sound and smell of Road Rash. Yes, I named my motorcycle. Please do call me crazy—I take it as a compliment. The bike is completely blacked out and more of a speeder than a cruiser, if you know what I mean.

Rosanna holds onto the rail behind the seat to hold on, and it arches her back. Now, I've been physically beaten up and mentally abused before, but none of it compares to the torture of not touching her right this second.

I reach behind me, grab her wrists, and place her arms across my chest. I don't like the idea of her holding onto something unsafe, or maybe I've convinced myself of that just to get her hands on my body. She leans in as I back up the bike, and I feel her warm chest against my back. The rapid rise and fall of her deep breaths. She's nervous, so I squeeze her thigh in comfort.

"You ready?" She nods in response. "Hold on tight."

I speed up so fast that the bike pops a small wheelie, making Rosie squeal and giggle in surprise. Taking the next turn sharply, our speed rises to seventy as we straighten out. We're speeding, but the cops in town know better than to pull me over.

When Rosie unexpectedly takes her palms off my chest, I immediately let go of the gas, causing the bike to jerk forward. I start to turn my head to tell her not to ever let go, but before I can, she leans forward and places her hands over mine on the handles. They're small, soft, with fingernails painted black, whereas mine are big and rough. She revs the gas, making the bike purr. *Atta girl.*

I steer while she controls the speed, which increases to about ninety, following the luckily empty and relatively straight road to Rosie's house.

I know everything about Rosanna Mariano, from her address to her favorite nail polish color.

As we reach a left turn up ahead, I take her hands one at a time and put them back on my chest. "Do not let go," I order firmly, and she nods in understanding.

Holding on tight to the handles, I twist the throttle. At the very last second, I push the brakes and lean low to the road, drifting into the turn. The roar of the motorcycle is music to my ears until I hear Rosie's echoing laugh. That is my new favorite melody.

I pull back on the gas as we approach her neighborhood, stopping a block away from her house. The Mariano family would not like me being with their daughter or her riding on my bike. Rosie dismounts, using my shoulder for balance, and slides the helmet off her head. Her hair is a disheveled wreck, and I love to see her unraveled. The woman doesn't have to always be so perfect.

She thrusts the helmet into my chest. "While I appreciate the ride, Rocco, you're still dead to me."

I grin while my rose walks away and turns to her parents' estate. Hate is good. Hate is passion, and I like hate.

CHAPTER 3

Rosanna

The motorcycle ride was full of adrenaline, and it may be my new addiction. Don't even get me started on feeling Rocco's abs. I mean, I had to hold onto something, right? But I'd rather be addicted to hardcore drugs than that man's presence. He's dangerous and could tarnish my reputation with a snap of his fingers.

"Evening, Al. I appreciate you waiting up for me." I say to the family butler. Alfred's been working for the Mariano family since I was a child, so he's like an uncle to me. After years of effort, I finally convinced him to help me sneak out. He could get fired for it, but he's an old friend who wants me to be happy and free now and then. Being a Mariano is exhausting, and it can suck the life out of you.

I'm so exhausted that the second I lie down in my bed, I crash into a deep slumber, dreaming of leather and black hair. Or would that be considered a nightmare?

FBGM Group Chat

Angelina: Anyone else in desperate need of a coffee?

Rosie: Omg. Yes, please.

Gia: If it means I get to look at your pretty faces, then hell to the yes!

Rosie: I would love to know how you have this much energy, hungover at seven a.m.

Gia: The sun is shining, my room is clean, and I slept like a baby. Plus, I love mornings. They're the start of a new day!

Angelina: I'll pick you up in thirty minutes. Gia, you're getting decaf.

Rosie: Thank God. Love you, GG, but multiply your energy by a hundred with coffee? No amount of caffeine or sleep could prepare me for that.

Gia: You two are so funny. I save coffee for the night anyway. Otherwise, I'd spend my days cleaning everything I look at. See you soon. Love you!

Rosie: Love you more.

Angelina: Love you more.

I stretch my arms above my head and sit up, trying to wake my body up from the very little sleep I got. As much as I love going out at night, and I'd never give up that side of myself, but it fucks with my sleep schedule. I'll have to sneak a nap in at some point today… If my parents let me. They don't particularly like naps. Apparently, I'm lazy and will gain weight if I stay in bed during the day. There are a lot of things about my life that they critique and complain about. They aren't nearly as controlling as Angelina's dad was, but that doesn't mean that I have freedom, either. My parents either want the best for me or the Mariano name. I can't seem to figure out which one it is.

After throwing on a pair of jeans, a distressed green top, and my black combat boots, I brush through my long black hair and promptly ignore the bags under my eyes for the time being.

Hoping to avoid my parents, I head downstairs and immediately fail. Both of them are in the kitchen, eating the breakfast the maid cooked. My mom lifts her head from her phone and says, "Morning, Rosanna, want to join us?" before I can get out the door.

Everyone says I look just like my mother when she was younger, and I guess I can kind of see it. She has shoulder-length black hair, but that's where our similarities end. Her eyes are brown, whereas mine are green. My mother, Cecilia Mariano, looks very good for her age, all thanks to her surgeons. She has tan skin, a sharp jawline, full lips, and not a single wrinkle in sight. My facial features look nothing like either of my parents. And honestly, thank God for that. My mom is gorgeous, but I prefer natural over fake.

"Thanks, Mom, but I'm meeting the girls for breakfast at Café Florian. I gotta go. I'm running late."

She makes a judgmental face. "Wearing that? Honey, your shirt looks like you got it from the Goodwill bin."

"It's supposed to look that way. It's in style."

"A Mariano doesn't dress like a hobo."

"Bye, Mom! Bye, Dad! Love you!" I yell, rushing out the door before she can make me change.

Of course, I didn't tell them that Angelina is picking me up. The last thing I need is for them to ask questions about the whereabouts of my car. I'll get it back before they notice.

When I walk around the block to her red Audi, I see both of my friends inside and smile. We drive to the coffee shop, blaring music, jamming out, and acting like a bunch of teenagers. Thanks to her father, Angelina didn't get to be a teenager, so we tend to make up for lost time whenever possible. He was controlling—homeschooling, constant supervision, no access to the outside world, etc. That is until everything went to shit when she got a boyfriend. Ultimately, I took care of the problem. Her father, that is.

Café Florian is one of our favorite spots to meet up. It's in a busy part of town, with an outdoor strip mall full of local boutiques, chain stores, and some of the best restaurants in Italy. That's not the best part, though. That's the bike rentals. I always choose the same one, a light blue bike with a woven basket. Angelina gets on the red one, and Gia picks the pink one with flowers all over it. Having a girls' day riding bikes, shopping at the mall, and getting coffee will never get old.

Our first stop is the coffee shop decorated with flowers and vines. Each table is adorned with unique vases of peonies, lilies, or roses, and bouquets of blooms available for purchase are placed everywhere in the room.

After we order drinks and pay for our chosen flowers, a single rose for me, we stand to the side to wait. The bell chimes above the door, and I turn my head on reflex. Instantly, I wish I had never looked. Standing in the threshold, in high heels and a preppy outfit, is Alex Bianchi. She's always hated us, even though we've done nothing to her. Hell, we do our best to avoid her, but she always finds us.

"I haven't seen her since graduation months ago. This could go one of two ways," Gia murmurs.

"I've never even met her, yet she hates me. What the hell did I do?" Angelina asks, even though she'll never get the answer. Alex hates people simply for getting what she wants, and she has always had her eyes on Nicolai. She made passes at him, flirted, and showed up at his club, but he always turned her down. So, it's safe to say that she hates my friend for getting the man she's pined after for years.

As for me and Gia, she hates us for being pretty. Alex was the most popular girl in our private school because she was the richest bitch, but we were popular for our looks. All the guys chased after us even though we weren't interested in young, entitled boys. Which is exactly what they were. When Gia gave one of them a chance, he pulled her heart out and stepped all over it.

Alex approaches our group with the fakest smile I've ever seen. "Omg, look who it is! I never thought I'd see you ladies again. How are you?"

My friends and I glance at each other with looks of confusion. Okay… So, maybe she's changed? Alex never bothered with niceties before.

"Alex, is it? It's nice to meet you. I'm Angelina."

Alex looks directly in her direction for the first time since she walked in. It's almost like she was pretending my friend wasn't there. "Yes, I've heard so much about you. I'm so sorry to hear about Mr. Vittori. How's your mom doing?"

"Good! She started a bakery here in town, and it has the best cupcakes. You should come by sometime. On the house!" Angelina is very kind, but give her a reason not to be, and she will fuck you up.

"That is so sweet! I'm afraid I don't eat carbs. Some of us watch our weight before it's too late."

This bitch just insinuated that my bestie's fat. If anything, Angelina is smaller than Alex.

Angelina giggles, "Right."

Alex's expression morphs from a fake smile to a resting bitch face, making my guard go up. She leans forward and whispers loud enough for us to hear, "You may have a bakery, a club, Italy's most eligible bachelor, but it's me he thinks about when he strokes himself at night while you're asleep."

She should know better than to speak about Angelina's husband like that. Nicolai warned us about Alex. She's crazy, and he never once slept with her or even gave her a chance. Angelina grabs Alex by her extensions and yanks hard, making her whine in pain.

"You will not speak about my husband again, or I will cut out your tongue. Do you know what happened to Mr. Vittori? I watched a bullet go through his skull, and I smiled when his lifeless eyes met mine. I'd watch where you tread, Alex, because you don't know who you're fucking with."

The bitch just stands there with a face full of shock, anger, and fear. The bell rings again, and Nicolai walks in. He walks up to Angelina, completely ignoring Alex, and shoves his tongue down his wife's throat. Gia and I make puking faces at each other. We love that they're happy, though.

Nicolai looks over her shoulder at us. "Mind if I borrow my wife for a bit?" He asks.

Gia points at him sternly. "Fine, but she owes us a shopping spree!"

"Deal." He hands me the keys to my Challenger. Angelina must have told him about my car troubles.

"Thank you. Go on. Take her away."

He throws Angelina over his shoulder and walks out the door without her coffee. All the while, Alex throws daggers at them with her eyes.

Gia and I grab our drinks, hoping to escape the inevitable fallout.

"Not so fast. She may get away with walking out of here, but like hell you are," Alex growls.

"What are you gonna do to stop me?"

Before I can dodge, she tips her cup over my head. Liquid spills down my hair, caramel sticks to my skin, and the ice freezes me to my core.

"What the fuck!?" Gia yells. She very rarely cusses so that's how I know shits about to go down, and I lift my hand to stop her from retaliating.

Alex turns to walk away, but I grip her arm and whip her body back around toward me. Before she can open her mouth, I slap her across the face so hard I can already see a handprint forming on her cheek.

"Next time, it'll be a gun instead of my hand, and I'm not afraid to knock you out with it and pull the trigger while you're unconscious."

"Is that a threat?"

I smirk. "Just a friendly suggestion to stay the fuck away from me and my friends."

"Whatever. Your handprint will be all over the media tomorrow, and everyone will see how crazy you are," she whines.

"Like I give a shit." I grab Gia, and we leave. I wasn't lying. I don't give a shit. The problem is that my parents do.

My friend and I shop around the town square for a few hours after I buy a change of clothes to clean up. I got black combat boots, even though I own similar ones, because they have unique buckles that drew me in the second I saw them. Gia splurged on a pink Gucci purse, and I almost bought the matching black one.

It's not until I'm driving Gia back home that she finally mentions what happened. "I can't believe she dumped coffee all over you and said all of those nasty things. Are you okay?"

"I'm good, GG, don't worry about me. Plus, it gave me an excuse to buy new clothes."

"Okay. What about your parents? Alex will run to social media, whining about the imprint on her face. I guarantee she'll twist the story, too."

"I'll survive. What's the worst they can do? Cut me off? I'll manage."

I know that I should be worried about the repercussions of my actions, but I'm not, and I don't regret it for a second. Alex deserved that hit, and I wasn't going to let her walk all over my friends and me.

I pull up to Gia's house, but she hesitates before she opens the door. "Please text me if you need anything at all. You can always stay here, you know?"

"Thank you. It won't come to that. My parents would never kick me out because that's exactly what I'd want. A life without the Mariano name constantly nagging at me? I wish." I stare out of the front windshield, zoned out and in my thoughts, imagining what that life would be like.

"Love you."

I reach over and give my bestie the best hug I can manage in the limited space of my car. "Love you more. I'll see you tonight."

When I'm alone, I give myself a second to breathe. Not that I can't breathe around Gia. I just need a second to myself. I lean my head back, close my eyes, and inhale and exhale until the weight lifts off my shoulders. Steady once more, I open my eyes and turn back onto the road toward my parents' house.

After I pull into the driveway, I hand my keys to our valet. No matter how many times I tell my parents I can park the car myself, they still complain that their daughter shouldn't have to.

I look up at my so-called home. It's modern and impressive in size, but bland. The exterior is a light grey California granite, with black window trims and a double-sided glass front door. The bushes around the estate are trimmed to perfection, and a black water fountain sits in the middle of the circular driveway next to the five-car garage.

"Good evening, Miss Mariano, I hope you had a splendid time shopping with Miss Leone and Miss Gabriele," Alfred greets me after I knock on the door.

"Evening, Al. How many times do I have to tell you not to call me Miss Mariano?"

"About as many times as the excuses you're about to make for what went down with Alex Bianchi," he quips back. Got me there.

I roll my eyes. "She started it."

"I don't think that matters to your parents."

Internally grumbling, I walk past him and into the kitchen. Might as well get this over with.

My father is reading the newspaper as usual, and my mom is sitting on the couch with her arms crossed, her foot tapping on the floor.

"I hope you enjoyed yourself, Rosanna, because you are grounded. Do you know how many followers Alex Bianchi has? After she posted a video of your act of violence, it has spread like wildfire!" She shrieks.

"She poured her coffee all over me!" I gesture toward my body and head, even though I bought new clothes, and my hair is now dry. "You can't expect me to do nothing! What if someone poured ice-cold liquid all over you in public?"

"I'd be the bigger person and walk away."

"Dad?" I ask, hoping for a smidge of support here.

"Your mother is right. As hard as it is to ignore people like Alex, we're Marianos. We can't afford violence being attached to our name."

"You're grounded. No shopping, no friends, no car," my mom adds.

"Whatever. I'm going to bed."

"Goodnight," my father calls out as I leave, defeated.

I walk into my suite and immediately get the shower running in the bathroom, eager to get the sticky feeling off my skin. As soon as the water is scalding hot, I scrub the caramel off and lather my wet hair in fancy, coconut-scented products until it feels like all the coffee is gone.

As I enter the bedroom, I stop short when I see something on my pillow. A note tied to a singular red rose.

To my sweet rose,

You may hate me, despise me, or even wish I were dead. But you can't deny the rush *you felt on my bike. Let me know if you need another ride. ;) -R*

How did he get into the house and past Al? Or know which bedroom is mine? How did my parents not see him, or me, for that matter? Regardless of my internal questions, he doesn't deserve my attention, so I throw the rose and the note away. I can't trust a man who could have gotten my best friend killed. Even if I could, my parents would never approve of him. Whether or not he makes me feel something, there are a million reasons it would never work.

I tuck myself into bed, turn my lamp off, and pretend to be passed out. Right on cue, my mom opens the door and peeks inside. Always at ten-thirty on the dot, she checks if I'm asleep. After she lightly shuts the door, I hear her footsteps go down the hall to the master bedroom.

As quiet as a mouse, I brush my hair, do my makeup, and change into a black dress. By the time I'm finished, it is past midnight, and my parents are guaranteed to be asleep. Both of them wake up at six in the morning, so they never stay up late.

Heels in my hand, I tiptoe downstairs and pass Alfred a hundred-dollar bill, as I sneak out the front door. I hand another hundred to the valet, and he hands me the keys to my car. My parents' employees are wrapped around my little finger, and without their help, I'm not sure I could leave at night.

Half an hour later, I pull into the La Citta del Peccato. Nicolai and Angelina are out on a date, and Gia said she had to clean her house, so I'm flying solo. The club is popping with people as usual. It smells like expensive perfume and cologne, with a hint of tobacco from the men smoking upstairs. I push through the crowd, denying men dances when they ask.

After subtly making sure no one is watching me, I slip around the velvet curtain under the stairway. People have peeked behind it before, but the uninformed are met with only a black wall. Unless you've been shown where the handle is, you won't find the hidden door or even know it exists. Standing on a chair, I rotate the light on the ceiling clockwise until it detaches, revealing a peephole to the VIP lounge. I *seriously* need to thank Nicolai. I pitched the idea to him, and the next day, he showed me the hole in the ceiling. No one in the VIP room can see it, but I can see them.

Tonight's suspects are Carlo D'Amico, Luca Moschelli, a few of their business partners, and a guy I don't recognize. He must be new; I would have remembered his blonde hair and accent. Americans don't come around here often, let alone to a club full of the Italian mafia.

"Are you married, Blade?" Carlo's always nosy about other people's lives, but for once it's not annoying. I am intrigued to know more about the stranger.

"Nope."

Carlo smirks. "Good. Keep it that way."

"Was planning on it," Blade retorts.

"You know, you should talk to my friend, Rocco. He can hook you up with jobs if you are bored with your, what did you call it, hacking?"

I highly doubt Rocco considers Carlo, who is twice his age, a friend.

Blade scans the room. "Sure. I wouldn't mind a side hustle. Where is he?"

"Fuck if I know. He's probably playing with his guns or drowning his dick in some heat."

The new guy nods. He may be acting nonchalant, but I can tell based on his body language and nervous leg tic that he wants to know more about Rocco.

"Oh, wait, he did mention something about a job down on Fifth Street tonight. Ole boy is probably hanging around in that area."

Luca hasn't said a word all night. He doesn't even look up at the other men surrounding him. All he does is stare at the blank wall, taking several absent-minded gulps of whisky. The way he's drinking, I'd be surprised if he doesn't black out tonight.

I almost feel bad, but deep down, a small part of Luca has to know that his brother deserved it. I wonder what is causing him to drink so heavily. The guilt of thinking his brother deserved to die, the relief he feels not having to cover up any more of Aimone's mistakes, or longing for the sibling he lost.

The men continue to talk about their wives, riches, and the game at hand. I'm not going to get anything good out of eavesdropping tonight, so I decide to indulge in my nagging curiosity and head to Fifth Street. After repeatedly driving down the same street back and forth, I finally found Rocco's bike. But what is he doing parked next to the Milan City Bank this late at night?

CHAPTER 4

Rocco

I've been watching the Milan City Bank for months, waiting for the perfect time to pounce. You know what I came up with? Nothing. Zero patience. I had a whole plan with my partner, Angelina, to rob the Milan bank in the daylight at gunpoint. Yet here I am at night, with a ski mask on by myself, holding a baseball bat, two duffel bags, and a backpack.

Bank robbing is not typically my thing. However, the bank owners of this bank are corrupt and take advantage of many people in desperate need of loans. Don't get me wrong, I'm all about corruption, if it's for a good reason. If you're using power to your advantage, though, we have a problem.

I've known the owners since my childhood. My father, the former mayor of Milan, had personal connections with them. Together, they would take people's unfortunate situations and make them worse. The borrowers were initially relieved to get a loan, but being in debt to my father or the Milan City Bank was digging their own grave. Even though my father is dead, the bank owners are still loan sharks. It's long past due for them to pay for their wrongdoings.

Patience? Not my middle name.

I swing the baseball bat at a glass window, shattering the barrier. As expected, the alarm goes off. I quickly rush to the security pad and enter the four-digit PIN that the bank manager uses every

morning. The blaring noise stops, but that doesn't

mean the police weren't notified. I have five

minutes tops to get what I need and leave.

I rush to the vault, enter another pin, and

spin the wheel to unlock the heavy door. As it

creaks open, I smile at the hidden treasure trove. It's

not going to be easy carrying all of this out. I start

throwing cash in one duffel bag, filling it with the

largest bills. In the second bag, I stuff as much

jewelry and gold coins as it can hold. *Two more*

minutes at most. I rip the backpack open and stack

gold bars in it. I strap the duffels across my chest

and attempt to lift the backpack, but drop it

immediately.

"Motherfucker. They make this look so much easier in the movies," I groan.

I'm not leaving this backpack here. With a deep breath, I think of a memory that makes me angry and gives me strength.

Rosanna on Aimone's lap? Yup, that'll do it.

Lifting the gold bars like they weigh nothing, I bolt out of the bank as fast as I can and immediately hear incoming sirens. But my parked bike is no longer where I left it. That is a big problem.

I look around, hoping I just forgot the parking spot, but it's nowhere in sight. As red and blue lights spark in the distance, a motorcycle roars down the road in my direction. It stops in front of me, and I don't even have to question who is driving Road Rash when I see silky, long black hair beneath my helmet.

"Rocco, get on the fucking bike!"

Right, that is probably a good idea considering the police are right behind us.

I swing my leg over, grab Rosie's waist, and she immediately revs the engine, speeding away from the sirens.

"Did you get my rose?!"

"What? Are you seriously asking me that right now?" she yells.

I merely smile and wait for her to answer my question.

"Yes, Rocco, I got your damn rose. That's not why I'm here."

"So, you just missed me then?" I run my nose along her neck to smell her sweet coconut scent, and her skin breaks out in goosebumps.

"No, you delusional psychopath. I was bored and heard someone say something about you down on Fifth Street. I was curious."

I'll take that as a more complicated way of saying she was thinking about me. "I thought you'd never been on a bike before me? How'd you learn to ride?"

"What if I told you someone taught me?"

"I'd tell you it's highly unlikely it was a girl, and in that case, he's a dead man walking."

She giggles. "Possessive much?"

My lips brush her ear. "I don't share."

Rosie turns her head to look behind us at the police cruiser riding our ass, and her face twists into an expression of recognition and confusion.

"Watch the road!" I yell right before we almost hit a car. She veers left quickly, avoiding the crash, and losing our tail at the same time.

She pulls to a stop in a dark alleyway and kills the lights to keep us hidden.

I jump off the bike and cross my arms. "What was that about? Where did you go back there?"

"The police officer who was tailing us was at Nicolai's club tonight."

"Yeah, and? Nico probably keeps them near in case of any trouble."

"No, he wasn't working. He was in the VIP lounge, playing cards and asking questions. Questions about you specifically."

I laugh, and she slaps my arm, but it doesn't hurt in the slightest.

"Rocco, this is not funny! You're being investigated!"

I shrug. "So what? I know my way out of these things."

She scoffs in disbelief.

"Aw, are you worried about me?"

"You wish."

"Sweetheart, if I could make a wish, it wouldn't be that. Trust me."

No, I wish she wouldn't take up so much of my thoughts all day, every day. Thinking about someone you want but can't have is consuming, exhausting, and aggravating. Rosie is too perfect, and I would damage her with my past and reputation.

"Tell me. Did another man teach you to ride my bike?" My gaze doesn't stray away from her eyes. I need to know if she's telling the truth.

"No, Rocco, I was just messing with you. I hotwired your bike and figured it out for myself. There's a brake pedal and a throttle. It's not that hard to figure out."

"How do you know how to hotwire a vehicle? You're a Mariano."

She smiles deviously. "Not at night."

CHAPTER 5

Rosanna

We wait in the alley for what feels like hours, but realistically speaking, it's only been thirty minutes.

Rocco's been gawking at me the whole time, and it's obnoxious, but a part of me would rather he stare than not look at all.

"Is there a reason you robbed a bank? New car? Perhaps a dream house on the market? Even if that's the case, knowing your lifestyle, you can afford it without the robbery."

"I didn't do it for the money."

I raise a brow. "So, why?"

"I don't expect you to understand."

"Try me."

"Long story short, the bank owners are pieces of shit who are using their elite profession to take advantage of the poor. Without any money, they'll have to shut down."

"Since when do you care about anyone other than yourself?"

Rocco shakes his head and moves closer until he's only a breath away. He raises one arm above my head, caging me against the wall.

"First off, I care about people who are taken advantage of. I know what it's like. Second, I'm not the selfish bastard you make me out to be. And third? I care about you a hell of a lot more than I care about me."

He's so much taller than me; even when I crane my neck, I barely meet his chin, but I meet his stare head-on. I've never stood so close to him before.

My eyes trail the vein bulging up his tattooed forearm before dropping to take in the black shirt stretched tight across his chest. I can see the outline of his abs, which I have to refrain from tracing with my fingers. His black cargo pants sit low on his waist, and he's wearing black combat boots similar to mine.

I slowly drag my gaze back up, and when I do, Rocco's grinning like the Cheshire cat. I suck in a sharp breath. How have I never noticed his eyes before? They're two different colors, and it's breathtaking. The left one is deep, umber-brown, and the right is sky blue.

His messy black hair has dark blue undertones, like the deepest parts of the ocean, and when he tilts his head, a few strands fall across his forehead. Almost unconsciously, I brush them back, lightly scratching my nails against his scalp. Rocco groans, and the sound is strained, like he's holding himself back. I slowly lower my hand to his cheek, and he leans into my touch. At this moment, I feel like I'm in an inescapable trance. We shouldn't be this close, I shouldn't be touching him, and he shouldn't make me feel butterflies in my belly, but I can't make myself walk away. Our gazes meet, and staring back at me is pure need. I fear my eyes mirror the same desperation.

The attraction between us is perilous, but right now, I'm too selfish to care about the repercussions. At least that's the excuse I tell myself when I grab his T-shirt and pull him toward me so our lips crash together. I'll allow myself this moment of selfishness because tomorrow morning, I'll have to go right back to being a Mariano.

Rocco's lips are warm and soft despite the chilly air surrounding us. When I part my lips, inviting him in, he doesn't hesitate to turn this into something more passionate.

"We should stop," I murmur.

"Mmmhm."

"I still hate you." I don't know if I'm trying to convince myself or him.

He smiles against my lips. "I hate you, too, sweetheart."

My knees weaken, and as soon as my legs start to give out, Rocco lifts me by the hips and slams me against the wall. My legs wrap around his torso, and he moves his hands under my thighs. He tastes like mint and smoke. Breathless, I break our kiss and moan his name as he ravages my neck.

"Again," he demands with a raspy voice.

"What?"

"Say my name like that again."

When I don't immediately comply, he grinds against me, and I can't stop his name from pouring out of my mouth. Rocco groans into my neck as a car drives by. The headlights blind me, a much-needed wake-up call to the situation I'm in.

Jarred back to reality, I push Rocco off and slap him across the face.

He touches his reddening cheek and then laughs maniacally.

"Don't you ever put your lips on mine again." There are a million reasons why I can't go around kissing Rocco Accardi. What is wrong with me?

He licks his lips as he stares at my mouth. "No promises, sweetheart."

I roll my eyes. "Let's pretend this never happened."

"You can."

"Look, I need to go home, and you need to get off the streets with that much cash and gold."

"Fine. But I'm driving."

He pulls the helmet over my head and straps it tight before handing me one duffel and keeping hold of the other bags. We hop on and the engine purrs to life. Luckily, despite the extra bulk, I can still reach around the backpack to hook my arms across his chest. Rocco takes off without warning, heading in the direction of my house.

"What about my car?!"

"I'll make sure it's back to you before morning! But right now, it's not a good idea to return to the bank. There will be cops camped out for at least another hour or two."

We pull up a block away from my house, and he kills the engine.

"This means nothing. Tonight was nothing, Rocco," I remind him as I dismount and remove the helmet.

He smirks. "Is that why you saved me? You're quite the getaway driver."

"I was just in the right place at the right time. Pure coincidence."

"Right. See you around, sweetheart."

"Stop calling me that!" I yell as he drives away.

I nod at Al as I walk through the front door, and he squints as if he can tell what I've been up to but doesn't question me. Suddenly drained after the night's unexpected events, I quietly tiptoe up the stairs and go to bed, getting a few hours of sleep before the sun rises.

CHAPTER 6

Rocco

She kissed me.

She kissed me.

She kissed me.

Rosie can deny it all she wants, but deep down, I'll always remember that she wanted me. I felt her body shiver and the racing of her pulse. I heard the sound of her voice moaning my name. I was a second away from breaking before she made the first move. I wanted her to want me, to be selfish for once, and to do something out of character. Now, she will lie awake at night and despise herself for that kiss. She will wonder what the hell she was thinking. And worst of all, she will hate herself for enjoying it.

I turn on the TV and flip through the news channels to get a different perspective on the day's top story. "Milan City Bank was robbed last night."

"City Bank forced to shut down after losing its funds."

"Suspect not found."

"Suspect is believed to be working with another."

It goes on and on for hours. I couldn't care less about the press. I'm just pleased that Milan City Bank is closed for business, and it can no longer take advantage of the poor and desperate. The stolen money and gold are stashed away in a safe. I have no use for it at the moment, but I'm sure one day I will.

My phone vibrates in my pocket.

Angelina: Are you kidding me? Please tell me that wasn't you. We had a plan!

Me: Plans can go to shit. Next time, I'll wait for your assistance. This time, I lost my patience.

I put my phone down and pluck a red rose from the vase sitting in the center of my kitchen island. On a small piece of paper, I write:

To my sweet rose,

I can't get you out of my head. -R

I attach the note to the pretty bloom with a ribbon and head to Rosie's house. Hiding in a corner where no one can see me, I text Alfred that

I'm waiting, and a minute later, he's striding towards me.

"Morning, Al. You know the drill." I pass him the rose, and he walks away.

You're going to think I'm crazy, but desperate times call for desperate measures, right? I threatened the Mariano family butler into putting flowers in my rose's room. I had no other way, alright? I'm good at sneaking around, but I'd rather not have to do that in a house full of security measures.

I spend the next few hours riding around town until I reach an abandoned park for a break. It's empty, that's the way I like it. Sometimes, the silence is just what I need.

The peace is broken when my phone vibrates.

Angelina: Meet me at the club in fifteen. And no, you can't say no. Nico will come and get you himself if you don't.

I get to the club sixteen minutes later, run into Nicolai, and put my arm around his shoulder. "Nico, my man. It's been too long. I fear our bromance is stretching thin."

"Good," he mumbles under his breath.

I gasp and place a hand over my heart. "How dare you? I'm heartbroken."

It's fun to mess with him. Even though he may not consider himself my friend, he's the only person who's ever come close to being one to me. A small part of me thinks that deep down, he enjoys my company even as he hates me for helping

kidnap Angelina. She's still trying to convince him

to warm up to me. I am her partner after all.

Not paying an iota of attention to me, he

plucks my arm off, and I glance over at what he is

staring at. Of course, he's looking at Angelina.

Nicolai always is. It's like she's all he sees. I used to

think it was ridiculous.

But lately, I've started to understand it.

Especially when Rosie moves to stand next to

Angelina. She's all I see. The music stops, the

movement around me is irrelevant, and it feels like

it's just us.

She's radiant in black skin-tight jeans,

combat boots, and a dark blue silky top that shows

the outline of her tits. I can tell she's trying to

ignore my presence, but she can't. I tilt my head, studying her until her forest green eyes finally meet mine. With a smirk, I give an exaggerated wink, making her cheeks turn pink, and she looks away.

"AHHH! Happy birthday! Happy birthday! Happy birthday!" Ginevra squeals as she runs to her friends, pulling Angelina into a bear hug.

I didn't know it was her birthday. It's not my responsibility, but I feel like a dick for not knowing. Damnit, Nico didn't mention it. We're going to have to go over the details of friendship at some point. Friends warn each other about other friends' birthdays.

While the girls catch up, I walk over to the bar and hand over my card to the bartender. "Start a tab in my name. I need five lemon drop shots, please."

A few minutes later, he sets the shots down in front of me.

"Thank you, kind sir. See those three ladies over there?" I point over my shoulder, and he nods. "Anything that they order tonight goes on my tab. Got it?"

"You got it. Enjoy your night."

"Thanks, man."

I pick up the tray of shots and walk back to the group, ushering Angelina away from the others.

"I apologize for not knowing it is your birthday." Nicolai watches us like he's about to slit my throat if I try anything with her. I would never do that. I'm not interested.

"I forgive you. I didn't expect you to know in the first place."

"Friends know each other's birthdays," I state with a frown.

She raises her eyebrows. "I thought we were just partners."

"I'd like it if we were friends, too."

She smiles. "Me, too."

"Shots on me!" I shout at the group.

We all raise a shot glass. "To Angelina!" everyone yells in unison.

My gaze finds Rosie's. I smirk, and we both tilt our heads back, our eyes never straying away from one another. She swallows the shot and makes no face of disgust at the liquor, and I can't deny how much it turns me on to see how good Rosie takes it. Most girls are babies about shots, Ginevra especially.

I wasn't prepared to drink and party tonight, but I would never refuse anyone on their birthday. When the girls go to the bar, I walk up to Nicolai. Like usual, he's watching Angelina like a hawk, and I can't blame him.

I still feel awful for helping kidnap her. Enzo Vittori was manipulative and persuasive. I couldn't refuse his cash offer after Nicolai dropped our contract, or the information he was willing to give me on multiple corrupt public officials. The second Angelina offered me a position as her partner, I was sold. I didn't want to be on the same side as her father, but I was backed into a corner, desperate for that information. Now that I know

Angelina, I would never, ever hurt her or take part in endangering her again. One of these days, Nicolai, Rosie, and everyone else will believe me. Until then, I'm happy to gain their trust.

"I'm sorry for not knowing your girl's birthday."

For once, he looks at me. Usually, he just ignores my presence. "I'm sorry for breaking our contract last year. I never had the chance to man up and own it. That was shitty of me to do."

I start to say something back, but he puts a hand up to stop me.

"Don't mistake my apology for forgiveness. You put her in a life-threatening situation, and it's gonna take a long time for me to forget that."

I nod. "Understood."

We shake hands, but I refuse to be professional, so I yank his arm and pull him in for a hug. He doesn't return the embrace, but at least he doesn't shoot me for pulling such a bold gesture. We step apart, and he straightens his suit right as the girls come back giddy and certainly tipsy.

Nicolai's establishment is Milan's most popular and exclusive club, but tonight the vibes are low. Which is upsetting because Angelina should have fun on her birthday. Everyone is sitting at tables, socializing, crowding the bar, or lounging out in the VIP section. Hardly anyone is on the dance floor. The girls notice, too, and Rosie walks up to the DJ, whispering something in his ear. A few seconds later, "LoveGame" by Lady Gaga plays over the speaker. Nicolai gives his DJ a warning look for playing pop, but the guy just shrugs his shoulders like it's out of his hands.

The song gets people moving to the beat, but not enough to be dancing. Angelina, Rosie, and Ginevra spread out around the club, pulling people to the dance floor. The club hasn't been so upbeat in months, and after tonight, the talk of the club on social media and through word of mouth will be good for Nicolai's business.

He gets dragged to the dance floor by his wife, and Rosie pulls me along, too. It doesn't take me much convincing. She can drag me anywhere she wants.

Nicolai doesn't dance. He never does unless Angelina is physically attached to his body, so he mostly just stands there with his arms crossed.

Me? I'll get down to some Lady Gaga.

All five of us converge into a tight-knit circle. Ginevra moves into the center and pulls a backhead bounce dance move. Angelina is next, and she does the Dougie perfectly; it's hilarious. I haven't laughed so much in my lifetime. She pulls Nico into the circle, and he doesn't look happy about it. But he gives minimal effort and pumps his hips to the beat with his hands raised to his head. Angelina eats it up.

Rosie takes center stage, and her dance feels like it's in slow motion. She turns away from me, giving me a view of her backside, holds her long hair up with both hands, and oh so slowly moves her hips to the beat. She undulates flawlessly, as smooth as butter. It's torture and the same exact move that made me notice her that first day in the club. I was in the VIP, and the second I saw her grinding with the other two girls, I couldn't tear my eyes away. She was completely oblivious to how enticing she looked.

Rosie makes eye contact with me over her shoulder, and before I know it, I'm pulled into the circle. Somehow, our tiny circle has grown. The people surrounding us are clapping and shouting at me to dance.

"Beat that," Rosie says with a wink.

I yank her close and whisper in her ear, "Next time you dance like that, it will be with me or else you won't dance at all."

She just smiles as if she knows exactly what she is doing.

"Either dance or get off the dance floor!" a stranger shouts in the distance.

"You asked me for it!" I walk backward and smirk at Rosie, who doesn't take her eyes off me.

I roll my shoulders and neck. Then, I drop to the ground, catching myself on my hands. I roll my hips and do the worm across the dance floor, making Rosie gawk open-mouthed at my muscles. Meanwhile, the crowd goes wild. The club has gone from boring to the craziest frat party any of us has ever been to.

"Best birthday ever!" Angelina shouts.

CHAPTER 7

Rosanna

I am drunk off my ass. This never happens. I'm always the responsible one. I take care of Angelina and Ginevra. Now, who's gonna take care of them? I am so stupid for getting this drunk, and I blame Rocco for it. He keeps buying us shots and drinks. And how can I possibly refuse my bestie's demands on her birthday? My parents just lifted my grounding after they realized I'm far too old for it. However, if they see me making a fool out of myself like this, I'm sure they'll find a way for me to reckon with my actions.

"I'm gonna take Angel out of here. She's gonna have alcohol poisoning if she drinks anymore. Do either of you need a ride home?" Nico asks.

Gia raises a hand in the air, and I shake my head. I can't go home like this, but I don't want him to worry about me, too. He has enough on his plate.

"You sure?" he asks me.

"I'm good. Thanks."

He nods before leaving with my friends, and the next thing I know, a deep voice says, "Aw, did you want to spend quality time with me? You could have just asked, sweetheart."

I let the alcohol do the talking because sober me would never say this aloud. "So what if I do?"

"Come on. I can tell you got more moves in you." Rocco pulls me with him to the crowded dance floor.

Rather than grinding on my ass like I expected, he dances in front of me. His hands are on my hips, and we sway to the music. Now and then, he busts out a move that has me laughing like I've never laughed before.

There's a tone of pride in his voice when he asks, "Who are you and what'd you do to Rosanna Mariano?"

I shrug my shoulders and smile. I hate to admit it, but I'm having so much fun with Rocco.

We spend what feels like hours dancing together. Some dance moves are slightly seductive, others are silly and childish. By the night's end, I'm laughing and smiling so hard my cheeks are sore. It's getting late, and the club closes soon.

"I'm gonna order an Uber home."

"No need. I'll take you."

I scoff, "Absolutely not. You've had just as many shots as I have."

"Actually, I haven't. I had one birthday shot and the rest were water."

I playfully hit his chest. "Are you shitting me?!"

"I shit you not."

"Next time, I won't let that slide."

"Very well. Now, can I take you home?"

"I would like that very much. Just one small problem," I giggle. "You'll have to sneak me in because my parents cannot see me like this. Oh God, could you imagine? I'd be shunned for life."

"That's inconvenient." He stands still, thinking. "Come home with me."

I laugh, but stop abruptly when I see that he's not joking. "Rocco, I am NOT having sex with you!"

"Wow, you're drunk," he laughs. "It's not like that, Rosie. You're plastered. I prefer my women sober."

"Okay. But don't you dare try anything!"

"Wouldn't dream of it."

Rocco has to carry me to the car because I keep tripping on air. I fall three times before he finally decides to throw me over his shoulder.

Once we get in the car, I pull out my phone to text my mom.

"No way. You cannot text your mom in this state. Let me." Rocco holds his hand out, and I surrender the cell to him. He's probably right.

He reads the text I had planned to send her aloud, "Mom! Hi, Mom! Hey! Just letting you know I'm coming home now. Rocco is driving me, but it's okay because he's totally sober!"

I giggle.

"How's this: Hey, Mom, it's getting late, so I'm staying the night at Gia's house. Love you!"

Not bad.

He drives the Challenger with ease as I sit back and zone out until we reach his house. It's not as big as my parents' place, and I like that. The house is completely blacked out, no color in sight. Even the windows are tinted.

"Let me guess. Black is your favorite color?"

He tucks a piece of my inky hair behind my ear. "Yeah. It's my favorite."

His heterochromia eyes meet mine, and I think he's going to kiss me. I'd let him. Right before he leans in, I feel something crawl up my stomach. I pull away, yank open my car door, and puke in the grass.

In seconds, he's at my side, holding my hair up and rubbing small circles on my back while I vomit some more. I want to cry. I hate being sick, especially in front of others.

"Go away. I don't want you to see me like this," I whine.

"I'm not going anywhere. You could be covered in puke, and I'd still think you're the prettiest girl in the room."

After upchucking three times, the feeling dies down.

"C'mon, let's go inside and get you to bed."

I've been dying to see what the inside of Rocco's house, but I'm far too tired to wander around. Plus, I probably won't remember anything tomorrow anyway. Rocco takes me straight to his bedroom and hands me a black T-shirt to sleep in. Like a gentleman, he turns around while I change before tucking me into bed, making sure my feet are covered.

He kisses my forehead. "Goodnight, sweet rose. If you need anything, I'll be next door."

I grab his arm before he can walk away.

"Stay."

"Rosie, you're sick and drunk. We're not doing this."

"Just to sleep," I murmur as my eyes shut. I'm so tired.

A few moments later, I hear the rustle of sheets and the other side of the bed dips down. Before I know it, I've fallen into a peaceful slumber until I'm awoken by screaming.

CHAPTER 8

Rocco

"I outta knock some sense into you, boy!"

my father yells.

"Please stop," I plead. I don't like begging,

but I'm desperate for the pain to stop.

"Accardis don't beg. They take." No, no, no.

I made him angry. I shouldn't have said please.

"When." Slap! "Are." Slap! "You." Slap!

"Gonna." Slap! "Learn!"

Blood drips from my lips as I fall to the floor

on my hands and knees. I take deep breaths, trying

to remain calm and let the moment pass, but I can't.

I inherited my father's temper, and for the first time

in my life, I can't hold it back.

Standing, my hands covered in gore, I meet my father's eyes and punch him in the face, making him stumble backward. He's speechless, so I take the chance to speak my mind. "You're a coward. You beat your wife so hard that she left us. But you don't stop there. You beat your kid, the only thing you have left, and then go back to pretending to be the world's best mayor. You're a liar and a phony."

He straightens back up with a split lip and laughs, "You fucking idiot. I will beat you senseless for what you just did."

His fist cracks against my cheek before I can block it, making my head ring. A kick to the gut knocks the wind from my lungs, and his elbow jabs into my eye socket. While I'm out of it, his hands circle my throat.

I want it to stop.

I want him to stop hitting me and start loving me like other fathers love their kids.

I want my mom to come back and take care of my cuts and bruises like a mother is supposed to.

Just once, I want to be told I'm not worthless, stupid, or weak.

I want to be loved.

"Stop! Make it stop!"

"Rocco! Wake up!" A beautiful, faint voice seems to speak in the distance. "Wake up!"

Ice-cold water jolts me awake. Breathless, heart racing, I look up in confusion. I had completely forgotten that Rosie stayed the night. I'm not used to sleeping with others.

She's teary-eyed and pale, as if she's seen a ghost.

"Hey. Hey, what's wrong?" My finger lightly grazes her cheek.

"I couldn't wake you. You were screaming, your body was shaking, and you were crying. I was so scared. I couldn't wake you. I couldn't—"

I pull her close. "Shhh. I'm okay, sweetheart. I'm okay and you're okay." I brush her hair with my fingers and don't let go.

"How often do you have nightmares?"

"Not as often as I used to. They come less frequently as time goes on," I reassure her.

"When did they start?"

I've never told anyone about my father. Not once. I'm not sure I'm ready to. My silence must be answer enough because she doesn't pry further.

"I have them too sometimes," she whispers.

Rosie has nightmares, too? Maybe she means the silly ones that normal people have about monsters under their beds.

It's like she reads my mind. "Not that kind."

"Why?"

"I don't regret killing Angelina's father. Not for a second. He was sucking the life out of her, hurting her emotionally and physically. She's my best friend, and I would do anything for her…" It's not easy for her to be vulnerable like this, but she continues anyway. "Just because I don't regret it, doesn't mean it doesn't haunt me. The blood, the high-pitched ringing in my ears, his eyes as he died, every second of that moment haunts me in my dreams."

Rosie opened up to me, so I'll open up for her. "The nightmares started when I was six. My father hit my mom for six years, and then, when she left us, he turned to me."

"He's dead now?"

"Yes. I killed him two years ago."

"How old are you?"

"Twenty-nine."

"Why did you wait so long to do it?"

"He was the mayor of Milan. I had to come up with a plan, and an escape route in case things went to shit. Honestly, I'm surprised my patience lasted that long."

"The mayor?" She asks in shock. "Your father was the mayor of Milan?"

I nod.

"Did no one notice your bruises?"

"No. He kept Mom and me pretty hidden, and when we had to make a public appearance, he would hit us in places covered by clothing."

"I'm so sorry, Rocco."

"The only good thing that came of him being my father is his connections to corruption. He knew every crooked cop, judge, public official, you name it. That information got me to where I am today and what I do."

"Why tell me any of this?"

"I trust you," I admit.

"But Rocco, I don't trust you. I don't know that I ever will."

I kiss the top of her hand. "It's okay. One day, you will. Until then, I'm not going anywhere."

She rolls her eyes. "I still hate you, you know."

"You can hate me all you want, sweetheart."

Hate is good. Hate is an emotion. Hate means she cares.

CHAPTER 9

Rosanna

Is it possible to hate someone and feel something for them at the same time? Before yesterday, I despised Rocco Accardi. I hated who he was and what he did to Angelina. A small part of me believed he was heartless, empty, and devoid of emotion. He took part in a kidnapping that could have killed my best friend. I can't just forgive and forget.

But I'll admit that things have changed between us. He's made me feel things no other guy has before. He's told me secrets about his past that could ruin him. Last night, he was vulnerable, open, and soft with me. I've never once seen him that way with anyone else. He gives me a million reasons to trust him, yet I'm still holding back, and he knows it. I don't know that I'll ever forgive Rocco, and for that, we will never work.

He is truly the most stunning man I've ever laid eyes on, and I didn't even think a guy could be beautiful. Handsome? Yes. Pretty? For sure. Cute? Oh yeah. None of those accurately describes Rocco. That man is beautiful in every sense.

He was visibly hesitant last night to open up to me about his past, and I can't blame him. I'm the same way. No one else knew about the nightmares, and I was planning on taking my secret to the grave, but then Rocco started screaming and shaking in his sleep.

I've never related to anything more. I don't trust him, but I instinctively knew he would understand, so I told him about my deepest secret. Some mornings, I wake up sweating, panting, crying, or even screaming into my pillow so I don't wake my parents. That night in the parking garage has haunted my dreams. It's not Angelina's father who haunts me, but rather my actions. I killed someone, I watched the life flicker out of his eyes, and I heard his last breath.

I'm one of the Whispers of Vice and Virtue. Killing shouldn't haunt me, but it does. I can't be the person to end someone's life. I will whisper in their ear, and torture them with my words, but to physically murder someone kills a part of me, too. I can't bear my nightmares. I'd get no sleep and go down a deep, dark mental hole. I won't kill again.

Aside from being woken up by Rocco's screaming, I slept better than I ever have, so I'm refreshed—but alone—when I wake up. A thick, velvet, cream-colored duvet keeps me warm, and I wish I could stay in this bed all day; it is so unbelievably comfortable.

When I finally drag myself up, I call Angelina and spend hours snooping around Rocco's home, yet I still feel like I haven't covered all of it. Past the front door is a spiral glass staircase leading to the second floor, and a black piano sits in the foyer, but Rocco said he doesn't play. I counted four bathrooms and eight bedrooms. When I asked why he has so many, he claimed he wants a big family.

With no mom, dad, aunts, uncles, cousins, or grandparents, it makes sense. Everyone deserves a family.

The spacious living room is dominated by a white, L-shaped couch in front of a marble fireplace, a 75-inch TV, and several gaming consoles. My favorite room in the house is the kitchen. It has two Dutch ovens, a microwave built into one of the cabinets, and an island. The best part? A lit coconut-scented candle sits on the countertop next to a cake stand full of cupcakes. I'd recognize those pastries anywhere. They're from Tori Vittori's bakery. She makes the best in all of Italy, I swear. I pop one into my mouth before I head back upstairs to find Rocco. As I step onto the second-floor landing, I spot him leaning against a

doorway.

I lick the icing off my fingers, and his eyes zone in

on the tip of the index finger I'm sucking on. "Oh.

There you are. I've been looking for you."

"I'm wherever you are. I can always find

you, Rosie. I'd find you in any room or place, with

or without lighting."

I swallow, ignoring the butterflies swarming

around in my stomach. "I have to go home."

He sighs, "I suppose you had to eventually. I

can take you."

"No, it's okay. My car is here, so I can drive

myself. Do you need a ride to your bike? You left it

at the club last night."

"No, but thank you, sweetheart. Someone is driving that back to me as we speak, so it'll be here shortly."

He makes me nervous, and I need to leave before I do something stupid. "Okay. See you later."

"'See you later?'" Rocco scoffs. I turn to walk away, but his voice follows me. "Is that what you think we are? On a 'see you later' level? Right."
Based on his fuming expression, I think I may have said the wrong thing.

"Fuck that," he whispers before I make it out the door. A hand on my bicep forces me to turn around.

"Roc—" I start to protest, but I don't get to finish his name before his lips crash against mine, and I bite his invading tongue. Instead of pulling away, he smiles against my lips. I should have known better. Rocco's a psychopath; of course, he loves a little pain. One of his hands squeezes my hip as he grips my neck, tilting my head upward to deepen the kiss. It's so good. A moan slips unbidden past my lips, and I hate myself for it. I have to stop this from going further. I have to be strong. I push at his chest, and he gets the message to stop.

Rocco steps back and shrugs his shoulders with a sly grin. "Sorry, sweetheart. I said no promises."

"We can't. No more. That was the last time. You're Rocco Accardi, and I am Rosanna Mariano. We..." I gesture between us. "...don't work."

"Feels like we work pretty well to me." He winks.

"Ugh," I groan and walk out the door.

I text my mom that I'm on my way home, and half an hour later, I pull into our driveway. A dark blue BMW I've never seen before is parked out front.

"Whose car is that?" I ask as I hand over my keys to the valet.

"I apologize. I am not inclined to say, Miss Mariano."

"Okaaaay."

I knock on the front door, and Al answers less than a second later, like he was waiting.

"Hey, Al. Everyone's acting pretty weird around here. They didn't brainwash you, too, did they?" I joke.

"Your parents are waiting for you in the dining room, Miss Mariano," he says with a serious tone. His eyes almost look sympathetic. What the hell is going on around here?

I slowly walk into the dining room, taking my time to prepare myself for whatever is to come.

My mom's face lights up with the biggest smile when she spots me. "Rosanna, welcome home! I'd like you to meet our guest." She gestures toward a man who stands up from his seat.

I suck in a breath when I get a good look at him. He's stunning. Short, spikey blonde hair, dark blue eyes, and a freshly shaven jaw. I can't help but notice that his biceps fill his navy suit well. One side of his mouth lifts in a smile, and he offers a hand to me.

"Rosanna Mariano," I greet him as we shake hands.

I'm not shocked that we have a guest. The Mariano family often has visitors. What does surprise me is that we've never had one this attractive.

"Leonardo Capponi." He raises my hand to his lips and kisses it. "The pleasure is all mine, Rosanna."

I'm not gonna lie, for a second there, I forgot my parents were in the room. I'm blushing from head to toe. My mom is positively beaming. "I'll make our plates! Raffaele, help me in the kitchen, would you?" She doesn't need my dad's help. She has never asked for it in the kitchen before because he knows nothing about cooking, but whatever.

If I'm going to have a one-on-one conversation with Leonardo, I should be polite and take the seat across from him, so he can meet my stare head-on.

"Tell me about yourself." His voice is smooth with a hint of an Italian accent.

"Okay. I enjoy shopping and going out. My favorite color is black, and I love roses. I like going for runs early in the morning, and I have two friends who mean the world to me. My favorite food—"

"Trust me, I'm interested in every single detail about you, but I could get that information from anyone. Tell me something you've never told anyone before." He leans in. "A secret."

I just met him, what makes him think I'd trust him so soon?

Leonardo notices my hesitance. "I get it. I'm a stranger. But your secret would go to the grave with me." He leans back, waiting patiently, but when I remain quiet, he offers a proposition. "Tell you what, a secret for a secret. I'll go first."

"My pa calls me Leonardo, like everyone else. But my ma called me Leo. After she passed, I haven't allowed anyone to call me that nickname. It hurts too much."

"Why are you telling me this?"

"Because I'd like for you to call me Leo."

"You don't even know me."

"No, but I'd like to know you more, and I think I'd like the way it sounds from you. It can be our thing."

I remain silent.

"Your turn," he reminds me.

Egged on, I whisper a confession quietly to ensure my parents can't hear. "Sometimes, I wish I weren't a Mariano." I look down at the table, unable to meet his eyes. I'm ashamed to admit it. I'm grateful for everything I have: my family, stable finances, home, all of it. But if I could trade this life for a peaceful, private one, I would.

Leonardo's finger lifts my chin. "What if I said I could change that?"

I don't understand what he means, and before I can think about it, my parents enter the room.

"This might be my best roast yet!" Mom exclaims, setting the plates down in front of us. They do look and smell heavenly.

"This looks amazing. Thank you, Mrs. Mariano. You must come over to my father's estate so he can make you his famous chicken parmesan. No chance it can beat this, though," Leonardo compliments.

"Please, call me Cecilia. We are so happy you could join us. You're always welcome."

As we eat our dinner, Leonardo holds a conversation with my mom and dad about anything and everything. They talk about my childhood, how my parents got to where they are now, their jobs and hobbies, all of it. I don't quite understand why he

wants to know so much about our family, and to be

frank, I'm losing patience. Does he work for the

press?

I set my silverware down on my plate with

enough force to cause their conversation to stop.

"Rosanna Mariano, that was rude," my mom

reprimands with disdain.

"What is going on here?"

My mother and father look at each other.

"I was going to wait until dessert, but I

suppose we can do this now." Leonardo stands and

approaches me, taking my hands in his. "Rosanna

Mariano, we just met, and you hardly know me, but

I know you and I want you. I will work every day of

my life to be what you need. I will provide for you,

love you, care for you, and be the best husband and father I can be."

Excuse me? Husband?

I glance at my mom, and her eyes are tearing up. I look back at Leonardo; he has an open box with a 4-carat diamond ring.

"Will you marry me?"

CHAPTER 10

Rocco

I'm in the middle of a phone call when I hear a knock on my front door. No one should be here this late, so I check my Ring camera. As soon as I see who it is, I end the call and rush to the door to open it.

"Rosie, are you okay?"

"Can I come in?"

"Yes. Of course. What's going on? It's late."

She walks past me and then turns around, holding her hand up in the air.

My eyes move to the rock on her ring finger.

I smile. "Is that inspiration? You know I would have gone with you, Rosie."

"No, Rocco. I'm engaged."

My smile fades, but it comes back when I start hysterically laughing. It disappears again when I realize she's not joking. "Like hell you're engaged."

"My parents arranged it," she states as if that makes this better. "Leonardo Capponi. His father owns a winery. He grew up in a good family," she adds as if I care about who he is.

She won't stop. Make it stop. Nothing I hear will make this better. She's not marrying him.

"He's a nice guy, Rocco."

"Nice?!" I cage her against the wall. "I know you. You don't want nice. You grew up with nice. It's all you've ever known." I tilt my head down, inches above her lips. "You don't want nice,

do you?"

Her green eyes meet mine, and she shakes

her head slowly.

"Am I nice?" I whisper, biting her earlobe.

She shakes her head again.

"What am I then?"

"You're…um…"

Rosie either can't focus or doesn't want to answer,

so I pinch her nipple through her shirt, making her

back arch. "Answer me."

"You're a fucking asshole is what you are.

You make me so goddamn angry! I came here as a

common courtesy to warn you before you saw it in

the papers, and somehow, you think you have a say

in it. I am engaged. Get over it." She walks away

toward the living room since I'm barricading the front door.

I shake my head in disbelief and run my tongue across my teeth. "Get over it? Not gonna happen, sweetheart."

I pick her up and throw her on top of the piano. Before she can protest, I grip the back of her neck and force her lips to mine.

I'm not stopping this time, and neither is Rosie.

She pulls my shirt off, and I rip hers in half. She can go home in one of mine. With fumbling fingers, she unbuttons my pants as I yank off her leggings.

Stepping back, I groan when I see her body in a matching black lacy set. My favorite color. Her breasts fill the bralette like they're dying to be freed from their restraints. So that's exactly what I do; I rip the bralette in half.

"Goddamnit, Rocco, you're destroying all of my clothes!" Rosie complains, but her legs tighten around my hips.

"Don't care." I lean down so my face is eye level with her breasts, and I lightly breathe on her nipples."My breath just made you quiver. Can you imagine what my tongue will do?"

I take a breast in my mouth, taking my time with it before moving on to the other. Licking, sucking, biting.

She arches into me and moans the most melodic, lustful sound. She pulls at my hair, forcing me to back up and meet her gaze.

"What do you want, Rosie? Whatever you want, I'll give it to you. Anything. Everything."

"I want all of you. Right now."

She doesn't have to tell me twice. I pull her panties off and lightly push at her chest, making her lie down flat on the piano. Kneeling at her feet, I slowly lick a path from her ankle to her inner thigh and then I kiss my way up to her glistening cunt. She shivers as I get closer. When my tongue finally meets her sweet heat, she's so delicious that I never want to stop. Rosie moans, pulls my hair, and screams my name as she unravels under my ministrations. Little does she know, I'm not done with her yet.

"You want all of me?"

"Yes," she moans.

I line up my cock up with her dripping center. "You asked for it, sweetheart." That's my only warning before I slam in deep.

She screams my name, and her nails leaving marks on my back as I fuck her ruthlessly. I should be gentle, easy, and nice. But I'm not, and that's the difference between me and Leonardo. I'm what she needs.

Her cunt is so tight that I barely fit, and I groan from the sensation. "Tell me something, Rosie."

"What?"

I fuck her harder. "Does Leonardo make you feel this way?"

She doesn't answer, so I stop my movements.

"No, no, he doesn't," she whimpers breathlessly.

I pull out, pick her up, and sit down on the bench. Rosie straddles my thighs and slowly sits down on my cock. It's torture, and she knows it. I push down on her shoulders, forcing her to take my full length.

"You said you wanted all of me. Take it."

She stops hesitating. At first, she rides me slowly, savoring the feeling. But that doesn't last long. She increases her pace, and her moans grow louder as her body begs for release. I've been holding on for dear life since the beginning, trying not to cum inside her.

I lean my forehead against her shoulder. "Please let me cum inside you. I don't think I can take no for an answer."

"Yes. I'm on birth control." Thank fuck.

I grab her hips and fuck her harder than I have all night. Her ring scratches my bicep. For a minute there, I forgot all about the engagement. I stop, and Rosie whines, seconds away from finishing.

"Take that off," I demand.

She looks down at her ring. "Or what?"

"Take it off or no orgasm for you, sweetheart."

She scoffs, "You're bluffing."

I slowly start to pull out, and it's torture.

"Fuck! Okay, okay." She pulls the ring off, and I throw it across the room.

"Atta girl." I slam back into her. "Fuck, Rosie." I can feel the beginnings of her orgasm as I give her what she needs. In bliss, she stares at the ceiling, bouncing on my cock as she meets my thrusts.

"Look at me or I stop."

She doesn't call my bluff this time and meets my eyes seconds before screaming my name and cumming all over my cock.

"Fucking hell, sweetheart," I groan, filling her up.

She immediately lifts herself off me, and I miss the feeling of being inside her body already.

Once Rosie's fully dressed and wearing my shirt, she walks over to the ring on the floor.

"Don't you dare," I growl.

She picks it up and slides it back onto her finger. "Rocco—"

"Don't. What was this? A quick fuck before you marry him? Wanted to test the waters and compare us?"

"No, of course not. I didn't plan for this to happen when I came over."

"Then why did you?!"

"I felt like you deserved to know, okay? Rocco, you have to understand. I need to marry Leonardo. You didn't see my parents' faces when he asked. I couldn't say no." She tries to reach for my arm, but I step out of the way.

"I think you should leave."

I don't even look at her as she walks out the door. I can't see her with another man's ring on her finger after what we did. She's supposed to be mine. And for a moment, I thought she was.

CHAPTER 11

Rosanna

I felt like shit when I woke up this morning. Half of me feels guilty for what I did with Rocco, and the other half of me feels guilty for enjoying it. I shouldn't have crossed the line like that. He thought I'd call off the engagement after what we did, but the world doesn't work that way. I don't live in some fairytale with a happily-ever-after.

I tie up my running shoes and rush down the stairs.

"Going for a run!" I yell to anyone in the house. It's ridiculously hot outside, but I go regardless. The smells and sights of nature never fail to calm me in the chaos that is my life. Some days, I run as early as six a.m. because it's the only thing that can calm me after a bad nightmare.

Before I start my run, Leonardo runs out of the front door. I didn't even know he was in the house. I'm wearing matching lilac purple leggings and a sports bra. It's more skin than I usually show, but it's too hot to run in a sweatshirt. Based on how his eyes roam my body, he likes what he sees.

"You're here early. Cake testing isn't for hours, you know."

"I know. I thought maybe you'd want someone to run with?" Wow, I didn't even notice that he's dressed in joggers and a tight-fit shirt.

"Can you keep up?" I lightly flirt, putting my hands on my hips and lifting a brow.

He shrugs his shoulders. "Guess you'll have to find out."

I take off without warning. "Ladies first!" I yell with a laugh.

"You brat!"

I take him through my routine route from my house to the local park. There's a beautiful running path surrounded by tall trees that loops around the lake. It's often empty this early in the morning.

Leonardo runs next to me the whole time. He never asks for a break or complains about the heat; surprisingly, he's pretty fun to run with. I slow down at the end of the path and stop for water. I chug a few gulps and glance over to see that Leonardo didn't bring anything to drink.

"Thirsty?"

"I'm alright. I can wait till we get back to your house," He pants, but I can tell he's parched.

"Quit being a gentleman and drink my damn water." I throw him the bottle, and I realize I just spoke informally to him. Marianos aren't supposed to talk that way. "Oh my gosh. I am so sorry. I didn't mean to be impolite. Please help yourself if you're thirsty."

The corner of his mouth lifts. "Rosanna, you don't have to do that with me. Be yourself. Fully. Completely. I want to marry you. Not some version your parents raised you to be."

That makes me smile.

Leonardo tilts the water bottle back and waterfalls it, so his mouth doesn't touch the rim. If it were Rocco, he wouldn't have hesitated to place his lips where mine were. *Why am I thinking about him right now?*

While he drinks, I spot movement behind him. A figure with a black hoodie pulled over their head. They're so far behind us, I can't see if it's a girl or a guy, or any hint of their face.

Leonardo notices my distraction and turns to look, too. "It's a little hot to be running in a hoodie."

"Yeah. Some people are self-conscious about their bodies, so I won't judge. C'mon, let's go," I say because I'm suddenly uncomfortable.

"Race you home!"

"Hey, no fair!" I yell as Leonardo gains distance ahead of me.

I beat him to my house, but just barely.

We're both doubled over and panting from giving it our all. When we can finally move our legs, we walk inside and are immediately greeted by my mom. Brunch fills the table, but eating food after that much exercise would make me barf.

"How was the run?"

"Your daughter gave me a run for my money, that's for sure," Leonardo states. "I'm going to head home and shower before the cake tasting, if that's alright."

"Nonsense! We have four different bathrooms in this house. No need for you to drive back and forth," my mom insists.

"Are you sure?"

"One thousand percent. There are towels in the bathroom, and if you need a change of clothes, my husband has a few things that are too small for him anyway."

"You are too kind."

"Rosanna, be a doll and show him to the guest bathroom upstairs."

I tilt my head in the direction of the stairs, and Leonardo follows me. "Here's the guest bathroom. Towels in the cabinet. Body wash and shampoo are already in the shower. My mom will bring up some clothes for you. Call my name if you need anything."

He kisses the top of my hand. "Thank you, Rosanna."

I blush and walk away to my bathroom to clean up, too. When I open the bathroom door and walk out, I run straight into Leonardo in the hallway. We stop and both stare at each other for what feels like hours. A towel is wrapped around his waist, so his abs are on full display, and his eyes roam to the top of my towel, where my tits are semi-covered.

"Did you, um, have a good shower?"

His voice comes out strained. "I did, thank you."

"Was it hot?" I clear my throat. "I mean the water. Was the water hot?" Jesus, Rosanna, pull it together.

"Yeah. Very."

I squeeze by him in the hall to get to my room and change into a flowy, burgundy dress. When I walk down the stairs, Leonardo is waiting for me. He's dressed in a grey suit, with a white button-up underneath. He smells fresh and looks handsome.

He holds out a hand for me to take and leans down to my ear. "You look beautiful."

"Thank you."

He opens up the passenger car door of his BMW for me and drives us to the cake tasting at Cupcake Heaven, Tori Vittori's bakery.

I turn on his radio, curious to hear what he listens to. "Whoa, Leonardo Capponi listens to rap? Who are you?"

"I'm full of surprises." He grins. "Also, call me Leo, remember?"

"Leo, right. Sorry, I forgot."

"Don't apologize. Never apologize to me."

We pull into the bakery parking lot, and I'm grinning from ear to ear. I am so excited; I love Cupcake Heaven and Angelina's mom. It's been too long since I've visited.

"Rosanna! Oh, my goodness, it has been way too long!" Tori yells, pulling me in for a squeeze as I walk through the door.

"I know. I've been having cupcake withdrawals! I missed you, too, Momma T."

Gia and I have been calling her Momma T ever since everything went down. After Enzo Vittori was out of the picture, she has been the best mother to Angelina.

"This must be your fiancé. I heard the news in the papers and couldn't believe it! I'm so happy for you," she gushes.

Leo holds out his hand. When Momma T takes it, she pulls him into a hug. It catches him off guard, and he laughs. "I'm Leonardo. It's nice to meet you, Mrs. Vittori. Rosanna wouldn't stop talking about your cupcakes the whole way here."

"It's just Tori. Come, follow me, and we will get your girl full of sugar."

We sit at a small, pink round table covered in a variety of cupcakes.

"All the flavors we have in the bakery are on this table. We can do any icing you'd like. I left bowls of that as well on the side. If you need anything at all, I'll be baking in the kitchen. Enjoy."

"Thank you!" I shout as she walks away.

"You pick first," Leo insists.

I look around at all of the options and end up picking a yellow cupcake. I take a bite and moan at the delicious flavor. Leo watches me the whole time. I almost forgot he has to try it, too. I was hogging the treat for a second there. I hold it out, expecting him to take it, but rather, he leans forward and takes a nibble out of it.

"Lemon. Gotta be top three."

"I don't indulge in sweets often, but holy shit that's good," he laughs.

I gasp. "Did my Leo just cuss? He would never."

He lifts an eyebrow and grins. "Your Leo, huh?"

"Um, I just meant you… I didn't mean to say you're mine per se—"

"Rosanna."

"Yes?"

"I'm yours."

Blushing, I nod toward the cupcakes. "Your turn."

He picks up a green one. What a weirdo. "Not bad, but not top three worthy."

When he holds it out to me, I bite it and almost spit it out. "Ew. Oh my God. Is that mint?" I hit his arm lightly. "Are you trying to poison me? That's disgusting!"

No offense to Momma T, I'm just not a fan of the mint in my cupcakes. If I wanted that, I'd just brush my teeth.

"Alright, how about we pick a cupcake that's not green?" I tease.

I choose a white one, thinking it's vanilla, and my eyes widen when I take a bite. Leo laughs at my obvious delight. He leans forward, so I extend the cupcake out for him as I swallow the delicious almond cake. I swear my taste buds had a party over that one.

"That's the one. Please, please agree with me on this or I'll have to say no at the altar," I plead.

"That's the one."

"Yes!"

We try a few more cupcakes until we can't eat any more, but the almond flavor is still the best.

Leo gestures toward my lip. "You have a little icing."

I wipe where he's pointing, but don't feel anything on my face. He laughs, leans forward, and wipes his thumb across my bottom lip. I stare up into his dark blue eyes. He leans forward slowly, almost as if he's giving me a chance to pull away. I don't.

He kisses me. It's sweet, tender, and perfect. Yet I can't help but wish he'd put his hand on my neck or slid his tongue down my throat. There's no passion. All I can think about is Rocco, and I hate it.

His forehead leans against mine, and he smiles. "You didn't have icing on your face. I just needed an excuse to do that."

Rocco wouldn't need an excuse. He does what he wants, when he wants. *Damnit, Rosanna. Get out of your head.*

We ordered the almond wedding cake and a variety of cupcakes before hugging Momma T goodbye, promising to visit again soon.

Leo drops me off in front of my parents' place, and I kiss him on the cheek before I hop out of the car. It's getting late, and he hasn't been home all day.

"Goodnight, Rosanna."

"Goodnight, Leo."

I do my routine of pretending to be asleep, and hours later, I sneak out once midnight hits. I meet the girls at the club, and they rush me. They've been blowing up my phone since they heard about the engagement, but I was waiting to tell them all the details in person.

"How are you engaged?"

"Who even is that guy?"

"Where'd you meet?"

"Why so soon?"

"My parents arranged it," I state, cutting off Gia and Angelina's endless questions.

"Ohhhh," they both say in unison as if it all makes sense.

"He's not so bad."

"Yeah, no kidding! He looks like a god!"

Gia shouts, and I laugh at her bluntness.

Angelina smiles. "As long as you're happy,

we are."

"I will be."

"Go do your thing. We will find you later,"

she says.

My thing. As in, spying on powerful mafia

men who would kill me in a heartbeat if I were

caught.

I walk toward the staircase and hear

something faint in the hallway. My curiosity doesn't

let me ignore it. I slowly creep toward the sound.

It's coming from one of the bathrooms, but the door

is cracked open.

"Yes, keep doing that," a girl moans.

I almost turn around, uninterested in their fuck fest until I hear something that I must have misheard. That can't be right.

"Leo," she moans.

"You feel so good." That's his voice. That's my Leo's voice.

It continues. Every time I hear her moan, "Leo," it's a punch to the gut.

I push the door open and see Leonardo Capponi fucking Alex Bianchi. His face goes pale.

He pulls out of her and scrambles to put his pants on. "Shit. Fuck. No, Rosanna, it's not—"

I turn around and walk out of the hallway, hoping he will leave me alone, but instead, he follows. I can't stop the tears from falling.

He grabs my arm."Rosanna—"

"What could you possibly have to say that makes that okay?"

"I'm sorry. I'm so sorry." He tries to hug me, but I don't wrap my arms around him.

"It's not the fact that you cheated. Because you know what? I did the day we got engaged," I admit. "But Alex Bianchi? I can never marry a man who would pursue a girl like that."

I glance over at the hallway, and Alex smiles at me. She knew I'd be here. She knew exactly what she was doing, leaving that door cracked.

"You let her call you Leo?" My voice cracks.

"I'm sorry. She kept saying it, and I was too distracted to notice. I don't know what I was thinking. Can you forgive me?"

"Can I forgive you? Are you serious right now?" I push him off me and walk away, flipping him off with my ring finger as I leave the club.

I stop by the bouncer on my way out. He knows I'm one of Angelina's best friends and listens whenever I need something.

"Leonardo Capponi. You know him?"

He nods silently.

"Don't let him out of that door until I leave this parking lot. Understood?"

He nods again in understanding.

I walk to my car, grab what I need, and approach Leonardo's BMW.

I lift the bat over my head and swing it at his windshield.

"ALEX!" *Swing.*

"FUCKING!" *Swing.*

"BIANCHI!" *Swing.*

I move to his driver's side window once the windshield is unsalvageable.

"YOU LYING, CHEATING PIECE OF SHIT!" *Swing.*

I do the same thing to Alex Bianchi's car, then fall onto the ground and break down in sobs.

"No one calls me Leo."

"I'm yours."

"Marry me."

"I'll care for you."

"I will love you."

How could I be so stupid?

CHAPTER 12

Rocco

I need something to distract me from thinking about Rosie. My mind is consumed with images of her laughing next to Leonardo. Wearing a white wedding dress for him, kissing him, fucking him, and I *spiral*. In a desperate need of a distraction, I call Angelina and tell her I need help with a kill. She and Nico leave the club immediately and pick me up. An hour later, we arrive at the destination.

"Whose house is this?" Angelina asks.

"Judge Ricci. Last week, he let a rapist walk free with no charge even though the scumbag was proven guilty."

"Are you fucking kidding me?!"

"Nope. Let's go," I grumble. Nico stays in the car lookout.

I've been watching Judge Ricci in my free time. He's divorced, and his kids have moved out, so he lives completely alone. He's also very out of shape. This should be a walk in the park.

Angelina picks the lock on the front door with her bobby pin, and we creep inside, guns in hand. We don't plan on using them, but we keep the weapons ready when we first break in as a precaution. My partner in crime and I prefer quieter, less messy methods of murder.

The judge is asleep in his bed when we tiptoe into the bedroom. Pressing a knife to his throat, I whisper, "Wakey, wakey."

He jolts awake and tries to scream, but I cover his mouth with a hand. "You move, and I will slit your throat, or my little friend over there will shoot."

He glances at my accomplice, who is standing in the corner of the room with a gun aimed at him.

I hold his arms down as Angelina ties them to the bedposts. "We're gonna ask you a few questions and you're going to answer without screaming. You scream, we shoot. Capisce?"

He nods.

"You let a rapist walk free. Why?"

"I have no idea what you're talking about."

The judge looks everywhere but at my eyes. He's a terrible liar.

"Don't play dumb with me. We don't have all night."

Angelina pushes the gun against his temple. That always speeds up the line of questioning.

"Alright, alright. The girls who testified, the witnesses… they were all lying!"

"What makes you think that?"

"Well, you saw what they were wearing. They asked for it. And then for them to take the men to court as if it were their fault… It's bullshit if you ask me. That's why I became a judge. To help the men who are wrongfully accused," he says as if it's that simple.

"I've heard enough." I slit his throat. It's messy, and the blood gets all over me, but I don't care.

"Hey, we could have gotten more information out of him!" Angelina whines.

"No. He's a liar, and he's delusional about what's right and wrong. My work here is done. Let's go."

An hour later, Nico drops me off at my car. He doesn't bring up the blood. He's used to seeing red after all. I drive home, and I'm in just as bad of a mood as I was in before. I thought a kill would help, but I guess not.

My mood doesn't let up until I walk through my front door and see the one girl I promised myself I'd stay away from. I can never keep my promises when it comes to Rosie.

Hurt and longing shine in her emerald-green eyes, and tears gather along her lower lashes. I pull her toward me and hold her for as long as she needs while her body trembles with gut-wrenching sobs. Every time I hear her choke and scream in agony, my heart cracks further and further down the middle. I rock her body back and forth.

"Shh. I'm here. I got you."

An hour or so later, her tears stop, and her breathing evens out. She rises, removing herself from my embrace, and sits crisscross applesauce in front of me. Rosie doesn't look me in the eyes when she speaks; rather, she only stares at the floor.

"Leonardo cheated on me. He fucked Alexandra Bianchi."

I shake my head. I don't know much about Alex Bianchi. All I've heard are warnings from Angelina about how she treated her in the cafe and the other two girls while they were in school. That told me plenty about her, though.

White-hot rage consumes me. I'm mad that he hurt her. Angry that he disappointed her. Furious that he took advantage of her time and heart. Pissed off because he took the one thing in this world that I care about and broke her. Rosie doesn't deserve this, and if I could take her pain away, I would in a heartbeat.

"I'm sorry, sweetheart. What do you need? I'll do anything to make this better," I tell her truthfully.

"I want to do something for myself. Not for my parents, or Leonardo, or even you. Something I want."

"Anything. You name it."

What she says next, I did not expect whatsoever. "Help me cut my hair."

I adore this side of her. When she is fearless, careless, and wholly Rosie Mariano. Not Rosanna Mariano, but Rosie.

"You got it, sweetheart." I turn and guide her to the master bathroom.

She sits crisscross applesauce on top of the marble countertop, in between the two sinks. I stand behind her, gather her hair, and pull it to the back to see the whole length.

"Wait. Will you still think I'm pretty if I don't have long hair?"

I chuckle. "Sweetheart, it doesn't matter what your hair looks like, whether you wear makeup, or the clothes you wear. To me, you'll always be the most beautiful girl in the room."

She cracks a small smile, and warmth seeps back into my heart.

"How much?"

She indicates with her hand where to cut.

"I've never done this. I can't promise you it will look good," I warn.

"I don't want perfect. I'm tired of being perfect."

I bring the scissors up to her hair. "You're sure?"

"I'm sure."

I start to cut, and her black hair falls to the ground at my feet.

After an hour and triple-checking that I cut every long piece, I'm finished. It's not perfect. The bottom is choppy, uneven, and rugged. The length stops above her shoulders, looking like a messy bob. But when I look at her in the mirror, Rosie's glowing and even more beautiful than I could have imagined.

"I thought I couldn't long for you any more than I already do. But now, seeing you like this?" I shake my head. "You have me in the palm of your hand, Rosie. I would do anything for you. Anything." I mean every word, and I don't stop there. "The other night, I stormed off because I wanted to mean more to you. I didn't want to be a pity fuck or a side piece. I wanted all of you, not just your body."

"Roc—"

"Let me finish, sweetheart. If I'm your second choice because Leonardo is out of the picture, then so be it. If you wanted him first, so be it. If you used me, then so fucking be it. Because I'm one lucky man to know you, let alone be wanted by you. I'll take whatever you can give me."

"Rocco, you mean so much more to me than that. I never once felt the feelings I felt for you with Leonardo. He never measured up to you, no matter how hard I tried to convince myself that he did. He didn't compare even in the slightest," she declares, and I'd be lying if I said it's not exactly what I wanted to hear.

I kiss her cheek and turn the shower on for her. While the water warms up, I wipe off the counter and sweep the floor. Rosie tries to pull my arm and take me into the shower with her, and it's goddamn tempting, but she's vulnerable from the day she's had. She needs to be cared for more than she needs to be fucked.

I made her a hot tea while she was washing off. The lavender flavor always calms me down and helps me sleep when I struggle, so hopefully, it'll help her, too. She has calmed down tremendously compared to when I first saw her, but she's still shaken up. Leonardo has blown up her phone with texts and calls, but she didn't answer any of them and blocked him instead.

While pouring her tea in the kitchen, I look out the window, feeling the sensation of being watched. My kitchen is full of more windows than walls, but they're tinted, and I live in a private

neighborhood, so I'm probably just being paranoid.

I look around, and then I see it. Someone is

crouched down by a bush, watching my house and

watching me. I squint my eyes to try and get a better

look, but it's useless.

Tea pours over my mug and burns my hand.

"Fuck!" I run over to the sink and put it under cold

water. As soon as it stops burning, I turn off the

faucet and walk outside. There's no one there. I

don't think I imagined it, but then again, I've

hallucinated before from my lack of sleep. I ignore

the twinge of doubt in my mind and walk back

inside to find Rosie. When I do, she's already fallen

asleep on my bed in one of my T-shirts. I double-

check the locks on the house and then quietly crawl

into bed with her, falling asleep a few minutes later.

I don't sleep peacefully. I never do.

"Ma?" I call as I walk up to her slowly.

She sits on the bed and stares at the wall, unblinking and barely breathing. She looks lifeless and hollow. There's blood on the bedsheets. I don't know what part of her it came from, and I don't ask.

I sit next to her. "Ma? Are you okay?"

She doesn't answer. It's as if she didn't hear me at all. This happens often. She disconnects from the world, and I can't bring her back. I get up and walk toward the door to leave. For the first time in a long time, she speaks. It's so quiet that I barely hear, but when I do, my heart sinks.

"I'm leaving, and can't take you with me."

I don't turn around and beg her to take me. I don't ask why she would leave me here. I don't speak at all because I know there's no convincing her. Soon, I'll be left alone with my worst nightmare, and I'm not sure how much longer I can hold onto my sanity.

I wake up screaming as Rosie holds me. I wish I didn't have nightmares, but I don't know how to stop them. My father scarred me, and scars stay with you forever.

CHAPTER 13

Rosanna

I leave Rocco's after breakfast.

Unfortunately, I can't stay longer. My parents are furious with me for multiple reasons. Reason number one: someone sent them pictures of me smashing Leonardo and Alex's car windows, and they had to pay the press to keep it off the media. Reason number two: calling off the engagement. Reason number three: not telling them where I was last night. Shall I go on?

I stare at the front door of my parents' house, unmoving.

"Are you gonna go in or just stand here all day?" Al asks.

"Depends. How mad are they?"

"Honest answer?"

I nod.

"On a scale of one to ten, probably nine. But when they see your hair, that number will go way up."

"Great. I shouldn't keep them waiting any longer."

I walk inside and am immediately met with yelling. Not at me, though.

"Cecilia, calm down," my father says.

"I'm not going to calm down! Leonardo is not going to take her back after what she did to his car! How are we going to fix this!?"

"You're not," I speak up. They both stop and look my way.

My mother screams. As in, an ear-splitting shriek, and then she starts crying. "Your hair! What happened to your beautiful hair!?"

I shrug my shoulders. "I cut it."

"I can't believe this. You will get extensions. You will apologize and take Leonardo back."

I stand my ground. "Mom, you can't be serious. I caught him fucking Alex Bianchi. I'm not marrying a man who treats me that way."

"Everyone makes mistakes. You need to have forgiveness in your heart, especially for someone of the Capponi family."

I laugh and look at my father. "Dad?"

"Your mother's right. I've made mistakes, and she has forgiven me. You need to do the same."

"You've made mistakes? What kind of mistakes?"

"I experimented with other women before I could see what was right in front of me."

This has to be some kind of sick prank. "Are you joking?"

They both shake their heads.

"We love each other and forgive one another, as should you," my mom insists.

Love is not cheating. Love is not being taken for granted. Love is not being with multiple women while you're married.

"You don't know what love is." I turn around and walk out as they continue yelling at me.

"You will be a Capponi, young lady!"

I flip both of my parents off before I walk through the front door.

I drive around for an hour, trying to calm down. I go through town, passing Café Florian, my old school, a few other local shops, and then the police station. That's when an idea comes to mind, and I pull into the parking lot.

"Can I help you?" the officer stationed at the front desk asks.

"Yes. I have information regarding Rocco Accardi." It's the only subject that will get me into his office without suspicion.

"One moment, please." The lady gets up and walks through a door, but her voice is still loud enough to hear. "A girl here says she has information about Mr. Accardi."

"Bring her in," a familiar male voice instructs.

After I'm escorted into an office, I put on a fake smile. "Rosanna Mariano, it's nice to meet you," I greet politely, holding out my hand to shake Blade's.

"Officer Coleson. Take a seat."

After the police chase, I looked him up online but couldn't see his face or body. He has unruly, wavy blonde hair, a medium build, and bright blue eyes.

"You have information about Rocco Accardi?" he prompts.

"Yes."

He eyes me carefully. "And you're telling me this, why?"

"He helped kidnap my best friend, so I want him locked up." That's not a complete lie.

"Do you have proof?"

"Unfortunately, no, but I know where he goes on most nights if you want to keep an eye on him."

Officer Coleson already knows where Rocco hangs out, but I have to give him some information, or else he will question the real reason I'm here.

"Go on."

"*La Citta del Peccato*. He sits in the VIP lounge and plays poker almost every night. You're sure to find him there."

He nods, seemingly pleased that I'm telling the truth, but displeased that he already knew that.

"Thank you for the information. It will be very helpful in our investigation." He stands up from his desk. "Is that all, Ms. Mariano?"

"Is there any chance you have a card I could take with me? In case more information comes up, and I need to contact you."

I noticed when I entered the room that he doesn't have any personal cards in the office, so he has to walk out to get one.

"Of course. Be right back." He walks out, leaving the door slightly ajar.

As soon as I see him turn the corner, I round the desk and open the drawers. One is full of pens, paper, snacks, and a picture of a young Coleson with a girl.

I pull open the bottom drawer and finally find what I need. It's full of files in alphabetical order. I immediately go to the A's and find Rocco Accardi. I glance up to ensure no one is coming and open the file. There are at least ten pages inside. There's no time to read, so I pull out my phone and snap photos. Once I've gotten them all, I slide the file back in place, shut the drawer, and run to the chair that I was previously sitting in. Just in time for Officer Coleson to push the door open and step inside.

He sends me a friendly smile. "Here you go. Feel free to contact me if you think of anything else."

"Will do. I appreciate your time. It was nice meeting you, Officer Coleson."

"You, too. Have a good afternoon."

I walk out of the police station, get in my car, and call Rocco.

He answers almost immediately. "Rosie.".

"Where are you?"

"Why? Miss me already?" he jokes.

"Rocco quit playing around. It's important."

"I'm at the club playing poker with Angelina."

"I'll be there in twenty." I hang up the phone and turn onto the road towards the club.

As I walk up the stairs to the VIP lounge, I hear all kinds of commotion.

"She cheated! No way she won three times in a row!"

Nicolai throws an old man against the wall. "She won fair and square. Watch your mouth and pay up."

The guy pulls hundreds out of his pocket and hands them over.

Angelina immediately lights up when she spots me. "Rosanna! Oh my God, your hair! I love it! Now I want short hair. This is so cute!" Nico gives her an "absolutely not" look. He loves her long hair and constantly runs his fingers through it.

"What are you doing here?" My bestie is giddy with her win. "Did you just see me kick all their asses?"

"I saw. I never doubt your skills. I'm here to talk to Rocco," I state.

"Oh, okay. I didn't know you guys knew each other that well."

"Yeah, I've run into him a few times here and there," I comment nonchalantly. I don't want anyone to know what Rocco and I have, especially the girl he kidnapped. I can't imagine she'd be okay with me being with him.

The man in question watches me the whole time I speak to my friend, grinning as if he knows we're talking about him.

"Angelina, I think your work here is done," Nico says.

"Fine," she groans. "I suppose I don't want to rob them of all they have." She follows him to his office, waving at me as she leaves.

Rocco crooks a finger at me, and I glance around the room to see who's here. They have no idea I know their deepest, darkest secrets.

When I'm close enough, he pulls my arm, forcing me to sit across his lap. I'll allow it, but only because it will give the other men the impression that I'm a stupid lapdog and not a spy. He leans toward my ear and whispers quietly enough so others can't hear, "It's about time you joined me up here instead of hiding away like I've seen you do. But I won't lie, I prefer having you all to myself in the dark corners. Did you come to play?"

"I don't play poker. I came to talk to you."

"Well, Ms. Mariano, I'm at your mercy."

"Officer Blade Coleson is investigating you."

"Yeah, you told me that already."

"No, you don't understand. You're in deep shit, Rocco. He has a file full of illegal activity that connects to you. He doesn't have proof, which is why you haven't been arrested, but he's pretty damn close to getting it."

"I'll handle it." He brushes it off like it's nothing.

"You'll handle it? That's it?"

He shrugs his shoulders.

"How are you going to 'handle it?'" I press.

"I know some people."

I scoff. "Of course you do. I mean, you did kidnap my best friend and get away with it, after all," I throw in his face. Seeing Angelina a second ago reminded me of it.

"I also helped her escape. So, in a way, I saved her life," he reasons.

"Stop gaslighting me."

"I don't think you realize that I would do or say anything for you to forgive me."

"Rocco, I can't. She's my best friend, and she could have died. How do you not realize the magnitude of your actions?"

"I fully understand what I did was wrong. It was a rash decision based on money, desperation, and wrong judgment. I spent countless days and nights preparing for Nicolai's new deal and partnership. I invested everything I had into it. Then he backed out as if it were nothing to him. I was hurt, and to be honest, I was angry. When Mr. Vittori approached me, he told me lies about Nico and promised me things I've worked my whole life for. He took advantage of me when I was vulnerable, and I completely fell for it. So, I helped him kidnap Angelina, and I will regret that decision for the rest of my life. Sweetheart, I am so sorry for putting her in that situation, and if I could take it back, I would in a heartbeat."

I did not expect him to apologize, and Rocco doesn't seem like the type to have regrets. Yet, based on his unwavering and solemn stare, I can tell he meant every word. While it may help to have an explanation for his actions, it doesn't excuse them.

"I appreciate your apology, and I can tell it's sincere. I'm sorry you have to live with that guilt for the rest of your life, but I'm not sorry enough to forgive and forget. I can't give my heart to a man who hurt someone I love."

Rocco nods, and his heartbreak is written all over his face. That's not what he wanted to hear, but I won't lie just to please him. He taps my thigh and starts to rise out of his chair, so I stand. "I have to go deal with Officer Coleson."

He's not the only one who is heartbroken. In a room full of bachelors, my eyes always find Rocco. My heart always beats a thousand miles a second for him. But my heart and my mind are going in two different directions. How could I possibly give my love to a man I don't trust?

CHAPTER 14

Rocco

I stare at the police station, crack my neck, and plaster on a smile before I walk through the glass doors. Of course, the first person I'm greeted by is Officer Coleson.

"Rocco Accardi. For what do we owe the pleasure?" he asks with a fake smile. Can't judge him for it, though, considering I am doing the same.

I raise my hand to shake his. "You must be Officer Coleson." He squeezes my palm with a little too much pressure for my liking.

"May I ask why you're here?"

Before I can answer, the Chief of Police rounds the corner. "I thought I heard a familiar voice! Man, it's good to see you. You've grown so much. Last I saw you, you were just a boy."

I've known the chief of police almost my whole life. My father often worked with him to clear his name and get away with far more than he should have. I'm sure he was aware of the abuse that went on in my childhood, but he was too greedy to concern himself with my safety. At one point, Angelina and I contemplated taking out the bastard, but after months of stalking, we saw that he wasn't a bad man. He was just desperate for money when he worked with my father, and I don't fault him for not helping me. In this world, it's every man for himself.

"I'm all grown up, what can I say?" I pull him in for a quick pat on the back. I don't like hugging people, but I need to butter him up and get him on my side.

"Let's go into my office to talk. Officer Coleson, would you mind getting us a cup of coffee?"

"Of course not. Be back shortly," he agrees with a tight smile.

I walk into the chief's office and take a seat in front of his desk.

"How are Marianne and the kids?" He's been with his wife for at least 30 years, and his children are in their teens.

"Doing good! Mari just went back to work a few years ago, and she's loving it. I love my kids, too, but they sure do age me well." He laughs, and I chuckle with him, even though I don't find him funny.

"That's great to hear. Well, I'm sure you have your hands full here, so I'll cut straight to the chase. One of your officers has information on me, and I don't appreciate my every move being watched and jotted down on file for speculation."

He leans forward and crosses his arms on the desk. "What exactly are you asking me to do?"

"I want my name cleared, my file thrown out, and Officer Coleson off my ass."

"How much?"

"Ten thousand."

"Make it twenty, and you can consider yourself the most goodie-two-shoes man in all of Italy." He always negotiates, so I low-balled him with ten. I would have given him fifty, but he's too blind by the zeros to realize what this deal is worth to me.

"Deal."

I called my bank in front of him and anonymously transferred over twenty thousand to the chief's account. I know he stays true to his word, so I don't worry about him taking my money and not keeping his end of the deal. He will have my name cleared within the next few hours.

Officer Coleson enters the room with two coffees in hand.

"Coleson, I want Mr. Accardi's name cleared. Burn the file, and you will no longer be bothering him. Is that clear?"

I look over at the man, and he is seething.

"Is that clear?" The chief asks again, louder this time.

"Yes, sir," he says, slamming the door on his way out.

"I will personally see to it that he follows my orders. Is that all you need?"

"Yes. I appreciate your time. It was great to see you again." The chief opens the door, and I smile as I walk out into the hallway.

"Don't be a stranger!"

I pass by Officer Coleson's office and quickly peek my head in. "I appreciate your help," I tease.

"You won't get away with this."

I wave goodbye. "I think I just did."

I hear his fist punch the wall. Well, that was easier than I thought. I guess my father's corruption was good for something after all.

CHAPTER 15

Rosanna

"Just twenty more minutes," I pant breathlessly as I run my regular path.

I've gone three miles already, but the reminder of running with Leonardo makes my lingering rage flare. I continue jogging regardless of my aching legs and feet. I've chugged all of my water already, and I'm sweating profusely.

I glance at the parking lot and see that same figure in a black hoodie. They're just standing there, with no car nearby, watching me. I don't know when they got here, but my gut tells me to leave immediately. If I keep following the path, I'll cross paths with them. I stop, put my hands on my hips, and pretend to take a drink of water while watching the figure over my bottle. I turn around and start walking in the opposite direction. When I look over my shoulder, the figure is moving toward me with their hands in their hoodie's pocket.

Nope, nope, nope. I don't like this, and neither does my gut. I bolt in the direction of my house as fast as I can. My legs want to give out, but I force them to keep going. After ten minutes of sprinting at full speed without looking back, my pursuer is nowhere to be seen. Regardless, I run the rest of the way home, watching my back the whole way.

When I get inside, I wobble to the fridge and chug the first water bottle I see.

"Rosanna, I can hear your heavy breathing from in here. You need to slow down when you run or you're going to pass out," my mom admonishes from the other room.

"I'm fine," I pant with the little breath I have left.

"Honey, have you talked to Leonardo?" She walks into the kitchen. "He feels awful for what he did. You two really should talk."

"Mom, drop it."

She gasps. "I forgot you did that to your hair. I'll never understand why you would do such a thing."

"I love it."

My father kisses the top of my head. "You're just as beautiful as always."

If you couldn't guess, I'm a daddy's girl, and you can't blame me for it with a critical mother like mine.

"Honey, don't lie to her." Case in point.

I roll my eyes as she walks away. "Call Leonardo!"

"Let it go, Mom!"

"When is she going to realize I won't marry him?" I ask my dad.

"Give her some time. She just worries about you. She wants to make sure you have a husband who will financially support you."

"And what about love, Dad? Does she not want me to be happy? To be with someone who wants me, and no one else?"

"Of course she does. We both do."

"I find that hard to believe from someone who cheated on their wife," I bite out.

He nods, refusing to meet my eyes. I struck a chord, but he's the one who made the mistake, so he needs to live with it. "Rosanna, I love your mom and would never make that same mistake again."

"You shouldn't have made it in the first place. I love you, Dad, but she shouldn't have stayed with you after you did that. If you need to experiment with other women in your marriage, then they're not your person.

"I was willing to marry Leonardo for convenience, family, and financial stability. I would have signed myself over to him for my future kids' sake and Mom's satisfaction. However, the second I caught him with Alex Bianchi, I knew our engagement was over. I've made mistakes. I don't fault him for making one, too, but I do fault him for who it was with. I refuse to marry a man interested in a bully like her."

"I understand. I want what's best for you, and so does your mother. Give her some time, and she will ease up. I'll try to talk to her."

"Thank you, Dad. I'm sorry the marriage didn't work out, but I promise you I can take care of myself."

"I never doubted it for a second. You were raised as a Mariano. We can do more than take care of ourselves."

He pulls me in for a hug, and I squeeze him back, making him wheeze as I tighten my grip. We've done this since I was a kid, and I'm sure he will let me bear hug him even in his eighties. I pull back and ask him the question that's been on my mind for the past few days. "Hey, Dad?"

He crosses his arms. "Oh, no. The batting eyelashes and pouting are never a good sign. What is it?"

"Can I get a bike?"

"Sure. You could use an upgrade from the one in the garage with training wheels."

"No, not that kind. I want a Kawasaki." I pray that he knows what that is and doesn't freak out.

"You want a motorcycle? You want me to buy my daughter a death trap?"

"I'll wear a helmet and be safe. Please, Dad. I never ask you for anything."

As surprising as it sounds, it's true. I hardly ever touch my allowance budget because there's nothing I want except for this.

He sighs, "You'll wear a helmet?"

"It'll be my second skin."

"You'll go the speed limit?"

I nod, even though I may bend that rule a time or two.

"You'll tell me I'm the best dad in the world?"

"Is that a yes?"

"Please don't make me regret this." He hands me his card.

I jump up and down in excitement. "You're the best dad in the world! Thank you! Thank you! Thank you!"

"When your mom asks, tell her you begged me until I couldn't take it anymore, so she thinks I had no other choice."

"You got it. Love you!" I yell as I run out the front door.

"Love you, too. Be safe!"

At the dealership, there are a few Harleys, Aprilias, Suzukis, and lastly, one Kawasaki. It's a Ninja H2, just like Rocco's, but a different color. Matte silver with hints of green. It has Battlax RS11 sport tires, LED lighting, and a mean growl when you start the engine. It's stunning, sharp, and perfect for me.

Of course, I bought the bike, along with a matching helmet. The visor is tinted, so you can't see my face through the glass. Leaving my car in the parking lot—Dad said he'd pick it up—I walk out to my new motorcycle. With a twist of the key, the bike's engine purrs, vibrating under me, and the smell of smoke and fuel fumes invades my nostrils. I love it.

I head to Rocco's place, eager to show him my new bike. But when I stop at the red light near his block, another motorcycle pulls up beside mine. I smile deviously when I see a familiar Kawasaki. *Perfect timing, Rocco.*

I rev the gas, challenging him to a race. He has no idea who I am, so I know he won't go easy on me. Rocco nods, lifts his hand in the air, and traces a circle with his finger, indicating one lap. I nod once, lean forward, and prepare to take off. We both watch the stoplight, waiting for it to turn green. The second the color changes, we speed off.

He got the head start, which isn't a surprise considering I'm still a little new to this whole bike thing, but I have no doubt I'll catch up.

I shift in my seat, push the pedal for more gas, and speed up. I'm so close behind him that I could touch his wheels if I wanted to. My speedometer reads seventy. The speed limit is fifty. I told my dad I wouldn't speed, but you only live once, and I'd like to have a fulfilling life, fearlessly doing what I want. It's time to live for me. While Rocco continues going straight, I brake and quickly veer left down an alley. We never said shortcuts were against the rules, so I take it. The road is old, bumpy brick, but luckily, it's deserted, so I don't have to worry about hitting anyone.

By the time I escape the alley, Rocco is behind me with seconds left to spare. I can see the stoplight less than a mile away. I speed up to ninety, gain some distance, and cross the green light, winning the race. Honestly, when I agreed to race Rocco, I didn't think I'd win, but here I am.

I park my bike on a deserted road nearby, and he follows me. He jumps off and throws his helmet down.

He's fuming. "Are you fucking joking? You cheated! A real man knows shortcuts are off limits."

I dismount, remove my helmet, and shake my hair out. Rocco is speechless. Like literally, mouth wide open and not breathing.

It's kind of funny, actually, and I crack a grin.

"Good thing I'm not a man, then."

"Did I just get my ass kicked by a girl?"

"I think you did."

He looks at my new ride. "Whose bike is that?"

"Mine."

"Road Rash, don't look. Daddy just wants to take a peek." He leans over to whisper to me, "He gets jealous." After a few moments of examining every detail, he exclaims, "Holy fuck, Rosie. This is a beauty."

"I know, right?"

He stalks toward me, herding my body back up against the bike until my ass hits the seat. "Do you have any idea what effect you have on me?"

I shake my head and lick my lips. His eyes darken as they track the movement.

"I was already borderline obsessed with you. You have a badass bike, fucked up hair, and a bad attitude. Knowing you just put me in my place? Fuck, Rosie, you have to stop, or I won't be able to let you go."

I pull on his leather jacket, and his rough hands grip my hips. His forehead drops to mine, and his breathing is labored. He's holding back.

"You want me?"

"No. I need you," he admits.

"Take me."

"Here?"

I nod. No one is around, the road is deserted, and the sun is going down, so it'll be dark soon.

Rocco leans in to kiss me, but I push against his chest before he can make contact.

"Your helmet."

"What?"

"I want you to wear your helmet while you fuck me."

"Sweetheart, keep saying things like that and I'll cum before we even get started."

He grabs the helmet, sliding it on as he saunters back. I look up to where his eyes would be, but all that stares back at me is my reflection. My face is flushed, my eyes are hooded, and my hair is a mess. I'm anything but perfect, which is precisely what I don't want to be. With Rocco, I'm not afraid to be myself. With him, I can be flawed, careless, and fun while the rest of the world expects perfection.

I kiss his neck as I tighten my legs around his hips, and I can feel his dick twitch and grow harder. A whimper slips past my lips. "Rocco."

"You know, when you say my name like that, you can get anything you want. Seems a little unfair, no? The chokehold you have on me?" His voice is huskier than usual because of the helmet.

"Please," I plead.

"On your knees, sweetheart. It's gonna take a lot more than 'please' to get what you want."

I drop to the pavement, and the rocks dig into my skin, but I couldn't care less about that right now.

"What are you waiting for? You'll earn what you're given."

His filthy mouth is drenching my panties, and I'm so turned on that I could orgasm within seconds if he just touched me.

I pull out his cock, and stroke it in one long pull. He groans, gripping the back of my bike for support. I kiss the tip, but before I can pull back, he pushes my head forward, making me take all of him. I gag as he hits the back of my throat, but I inhale and exhale through my nose to breathe through it. I wish I could say I hate his primal instincts or the disrespect, but the truth is, it's exactly what I want. Everyone walks on eggshells around me except for Rocco. He's not afraid to be dominant, and I love it.

"Such a tease. I'm not a patient man, Rosie. Now, suck it like you mean it."

His hand fists in my short hair, and he pulls back so my mouth is only wrapped around the thick tip of his dick. He looks down, and in the visor of his helmet, I see my reflection. My mascara is smeared, my lipstick is gone, and my eyes are glossy. I'm a mess, and Rocco doesn't seem to care one bit. Without warning, he shoves his hips forward. I take all of his length as deep as I physically can. I teasingly swirl my tongue and grab his balls, tasting pre-cum.

He pulls my hair again and lifts me, ripping my clothes off and dropping me onto his bike. "I think you've earned my cock, what do you think?"

"I think if you don't fuck me in five seconds, I'll do it myself." I lean back on the bike, pushing my tits out. "Five. Four." I hook my legs behind his ass and pull him forward. "Three." I roll my nipple between my fingers and pinch. "Two." My hand reaches down to rub my clit. "One." Rocco growls my name as he rams his length in deep, making me cry out. "Goddamnit, Rosie, the more I fuck you, the more I grow addicted. I want to wake up inside you, take you in the shower, and make love to you at night. You'd never have a moment alone if you were mine."

He fucks me hard, with my ass on the edge of the seat and his tattooed arms holding me steady. I moan his name as my orgasm builds, but he pulls out before I can fall off the edge. I whine, trying to nudge him back inside. He yanks his helmet off and throws it on the ground. His wavy, black hair is a total wreck, and his eyes are darker than the night sky as they stare into mine.

"I need a taste." That's the only warning I get before he gets down on his knees and ravages my pussy with his mouth.

"Fuck, Rocco, keep doing that," I beg. I grab his hair, desperate for something to hold onto. I grind my hips against his mouth, moving at the pace I need. His hands knead my breasts, and then he pinches my nipple between his fingers, making me lose all control.

"Just like that." I move faster against his mouth. "Don't stop." I grab my breasts and squeeze, overwhelmed with ecstasy. "Yes, Rocco. Holy fuck."

I moan his name repeatedly as I ride out my orgasm. He doesn't stop until I'm completely satisfied.

Rocco stands, grips the back of my neck, and slams his lips against mine. I moan, tasting myself on his tongue as he shoves two fingers into my pussy, and I'm so wet I can hear each movement.

"Fuck, sweetheart, you're dripping all over me." He removes his fingers and taps them against my mouth. "Taste how delicious you are. I'll never get enough."

I moan again at the sweet and salty flavor. "I thought you weren't patient?"

"I'm not."

"Then why isn't your dick inside me?"

"Sweetheart, you're more impatient than I am. You'll take what I give you and thank me for it. Understood?"

He slides his hard cock across my wet heat, and I'd give anything for him to put it inside me immediately.

"Is that understood, Rosanna?"

"Yes," I pant, lifting my hips. I try to push Rocco in, but he backs up.

"Where are your manners?"

I will dream of this man's filthy mouth and fuck my fingers while thinking of him for the rest of my life.

"Please give me your cock, Rocco." I kiss and lick my way up his neck.

That does it. His dick goes as deep into my pussy as it can fit. I want more. I need more. I slide down so my back is on the bike seat, fully exposing myself to him. He fucks me harder and deeper from this angle and I can't stop the second orgasm from crashing through me even if I wanted to.

"Oh god!"

"You take my cock so well." He pounds into me harder and faster. "Sweetheart, I'm gonna cum. Please don't make me pull out. Fuck, baby, please."

"If you don't cum inside me right now, I'll make you fuck me again until you do."

Rocco immediately finishes. When he pulls his dick out, a few beads of cum drip out of me, and he slides it back in with two fingers, making me

shudder.

"Just the sight of my cum dripping all over

you has me growing hard all over again. I could

fuck you all day."

"As much as I'd love to do that again, I have

places to be." I get dressed and pull my helmet back

over my head.

"Forgive me."

"What?"

"Forgive me and be mine," he begs.

"You know I can't do that." Just because we

fucked doesn't mean I forgive him for his

wrongdoings.

I drive off before he can plead with me

more. I worry that one of these days, I'll cave and

give myself over to Rocco. I fear that I'll give him

my trust and have it broken all over again.

CHAPTER 16

Rocco

When is Rosie going to forgive me? What does she want me to do? I would do anything for her. Doesn't she know that by now?

Every time I see that woman, I want more. I want her to stay and cuddle me. I want to whisper in her ear that I love her. I want to spoil her and show her how much I adore her. Call me sappy, but I'm a lovesick fool for that girl.

I'm speeding down the road, trying to find out where she went, but her bike is nowhere to be found. She's quick and sure knows how to drive. When she kicked my ass, I wasn't impressed. I was speechless. I've raced plenty of people before, and none of them have been able to beat me. Then again, I'm not that surprised. Rosie can do anything she puts her mind to.

Right as I'm about to slow down my speed, I see red and blue lights flash behind me and hear a siren. Well, this is inconvenient. I pull over to the curb and park my bike. Minutes later, a police officer walks up beside me. As if he is trying to ruin my night, Officer Coleson smirks down at me. He is the last cop I was hoping to see. I could get out of this situation with literally anyone else, but Coleson? The guy is a prick. Honestly, if I knew he was the one pulling me over, I would have sped away. He rests a hand on his gun, clearly trying to silently threaten me.

"Mr. Accardi, do you know how fast you were going back there?"

"I apologize. I was trying to catch up with someone. I wasn't aware I was going over the limit."

"Right." He doesn't believe me for a second.

"Look, why don't you take this, and we'll call it a night? It's about how much a ticket costs anyway." I try to offer him three hundred in cash.

His tone turns accusatory. "Are you bribing a police officer?"

"Not at all, Officer Coleson." He doesn't take the cash, so I put it back in my pocket.

He leans in and inhales as if he's smelling me.

"Have you been drinking?"

Okay, now he's just being an asshole.

"Absolutely not. Feel free to test my breath, and I'll prove it."

"Unfortunately, I don't have my breathalyzer on me, and based on your speed and reckless driving, you're going to have to come with me."

I laugh, but he doesn't even crack a smile. "You're serious?"

"Do not question my authority." God, this guy's ego is annoying as hell.

"Alright, Officer Coleson. I'll go down to the station with you. Lock me up, ask me questions, and do as you wish. But let me tell you something. Your boss? I've known him longer than you have, and we're close friends. I can promise he won't be happy once he finds out you're causing me trouble."

"Put your hands behind your back."

He cuffs me and pulls them so tight that they dig into my wrists. He pulls on the chain, leading me to his car.

"Aren't you going to tell me my rights, officer?"

"Don't feel like it."

Wow, what a polite *cop*.

Coleson drives to the station, but no part of me is freaking out. I know this will be over soon and that he can't charge me without proof. He's wasting my time, but I don't mind it if I get to push his buttons and piss him off. Why does he hate my guts? I'll never know, and I don't care enough to ask about his petty personal grudge.

I sit in the back seat of his Dodge Charger behind the caged fence and tap my fingers against my thighs, suffering in silence. "Would you mind turning up the radio?"

"No."

"Someone woke up on the wrong side of the bed this morning," I mutter. "Do you have an auxiliary cord? I have some good songs saved on Spotify."

"No."

"MP3 player? Headphones? CD? C'mon, man, you gotta give me something." I don't really want something to listen to. I just enjoy pushing his buttons.

"No."

"Buzzkill."

After fifteen minutes of silence, he pulls into the station. I was hoping another officer was on duty, but it looks like it's just Coleson tonight, which is very unfortunate for me. He walks me into the station and places me inside a jail cell.

"We're keeping you overnight for alcohol use and recklessness."

"You mean you're keeping me? Because if any other officer was here, I'd walk out of the station, and you'd have your tail between your legs for putting me here in the first place."

"It's proper protocol."

"Yeah, okay. So, what, you're gonna spend the night with me? I gotta tell you, Blade, I have nightmares, so don't go soft on me now."

"It's Officer Coleson to you."

"So cocky," I whisper.

"What was that?"

I cough. "Coffee. I was just asking if you have any coffee."

"Yes." He doesn't move from where he sits at his desk.

"Can I have a cup?"

"No."

I bang my head against the jail cell. It's gonna be a long night. I fall asleep on the concrete floor hours later, but I don't stay unconscious for long.

Someone kicks my stomach. "Wake up!" Another kick. "Wake the fuck up!"

I open my eyes abruptly and spot two large, muscular men in orange jumpsuits. Don't get me wrong, I'm a big guy. I lift weights, eat plenty of protein, and work for my body. But these guys? I guarantee they take steroids for breakfast, lunch, and dinner. I look around for Officer Coleson, and he's nowhere to be seen, but these guys had to get into my jail cell somehow. I am in deep shit.

"Hey! How's it going?" I plaster on the best smile I can and try to pull one of them in for a dab, but it's not reciprocated. Okay, new approach. "I gotta say you guys are jacked. I mean, seriously, I dream of having biceps like that." Fuck. *None* of this is working.

"We have a message for you." They both crack their knuckles and necks. That is never a good sign. I know what's coming.

"Look, I don't want any trouble. I can pay you! Whatever they're paying, I'll double it!"

"This is for Lucy."

"Who the fuck is Lucy?" I ask, but I don't get an answer before a fist to the nose shuts me up.

The guy didn't break it, but I can feel blood gushing down my face. I try to wipe the gore off, but instead, it just smears all over the place. I'm done being the nice guy.

I try to kick the one on the left, but before I can, the guy on the right grabs my leg. He twists it at an uncomfortable angle, making me yell in agony and fall over. I can't fight them properly in handcuffs, especially when my two attackers are triple my size.

I'm kicked in the stomach again so hard that my body moves across the floor. I cough up blood. The last time I was this weak was when I was just a boy.

It's bringing back memories I don't want to resurface. Things that should only appear in my nightmares. Thoughts that I promised myself I'd never think again. A certain man who caused me trauma that will stick with me no matter where I go. And reminders of things I did that I'm not proud of. It's times like these that I wish I were dead.

"You're sixteen years old now. You need to start acting like a man," my father says.

"I don't want to."

There's a hooker on the bed. She's way older than I am and more experienced. This is my first time meeting her. I don't want my first time to be with a stranger. I want it to be with someone I care about. Someone who loves me.

"Too fucking bad. My son is not going to be a virgin, and you can't get laid."

That's because I don't have any friends. Nobody talks to me at school. They think I'm a freak.

"Please don't make me."

He nods at the barely dressed hooker, who saunters towards me. She's wearing too much lip gloss and makeup. Her hair is sticky from hairspray. She smells like cigarettes. I can't do this. I can't do this. I can't.

She tries to kiss me. I look away. My father rises out of his chair and slaps me across the face.

He puts one hand on my jaw, forcing me to look at her, and the other on my shoulder to keep me seated. I can't stop this from happening. I never can.

He made me hit her. He said it was me or her, and I chose selfishly. He forced my hand to feel her lady parts. When I cried, he made her suck me off for doing a "bad job."

I lost my virginity that night, and my father watched until he was certain I finished. He gave me a pat on the back and congratulated me, but I didn't feel like congratulations were in order.

That wasn't me that night. My thoughts became so loud that I had to turn them off. I lost my humanity, and I don't deserve to get it back.

That's one of my worst memories. Not because of the abuse I endured, but for what I did. After that night, it took years to pull myself out of the depressed, vegetative state I was in. I have to live with that guilt for the rest of my life. No hooker should have to endure abuse, no matter how much they're paid.

The guys left, and I'm curled up on the ground in a fetal position, but no tears fall. My body is covered in forming bruises, and the ground is soaked with my blood. I can handle it. I've been in worse condition.

A big part of me wishes they finished the job and killed me, ending my suffering once and for all. The thoughts, memories, and trauma never stop. I can't sleep, have a moment of peace, or feel absolute happiness without feeling like I don't deserve it.

But a small part of me wants to live. It's what keeps me breathing. It's the reason I'm still alive. Rosie is the only person who can make me feel like I deserve a happy, fulfilling life. She makes me feel loved, and I didn't think I was lovable.

Is that small part enough? Right now, I feel like nothing can stop me from letting go of my humanity once again.

CHAPTER 17

Rosanna

My ringing phone wakes me up. I have two missed calls from Angelina and one from Rocco. I call Angelina back first, and she immediately picks up.

"Hey, is everything okay?"

"Hey. I hate to wake you up with bad news, but Rocco was arrested last night. He got beaten up in the cell. Nico picked him up from the station early this morning." I grab my keys and run out the door before she even finishes speaking.

"He's at our house now, and he's asking for you. He's in bad shape, Rose."

"I'm on my way."

I end the call and speed to their house. My breathing is ragged, and my hands shake. How badly was he beaten up? Is he okay? What the hell happened after I left last night?

I pull into the driveway, jump off my bike, and head in, not even bothering to knock before I enter.

"Where is he?"

Angelina just points to a second-floor guest room, and I bound up the stairs.

Rocco is curled up in bed. He doesn't even move when I walk in. I thought he might be sleeping, but his eyes are open, staring at the wall. He looks broken.

"Rocco?" I brush the hair out of his face. His gaze is hollow and lifeless. He's not okay mentally, let alone physically. Yellow bruises cover his body, dry blood is caked on his skin, and his clothes are dirty from sleeping in a jail cell all night.

I don't know what to do. He won't even look at me. He's not himself.

"Do you want me to leave?" I don't want to invade his space.

He shakes his head no.

"Okay, I'll stay. I'm gonna hold you. If you don't want me to, then just pull away."

I lay down next to him, wrap my arms around his waist, and lay my cheek on his neck. Absentmindedly, I play with his wavy locks and quietly sing "J's Lullaby" by Delaney Bailey. I'm not a good singer, but he doesn't seem to mind.

When I finish singing, I see a faint tear drop from his eye. I wipe it away and kiss where it used to be. "You're okay. Come back to me."

After some time, Angelina texted me that she and Nico were going out. The house is silent except for the sound of my singing and humming.

I spend the entire day whispering sweet nothings into Rocco's ear. When the sun goes down, he finally turns around and meets my eyes. It may be small, but I see light in his irises. I lean in and lightly kiss his lips.

"I'm sorry," he whispers.

"Why are you apologizing?"

"Because you deserve better than me, but I can't find it in myself to let you go."

"Rocco, you deserve the world. I wish I could give it to you and make this all better, but you know I can't do that. What happened last night?"

"Officer Coleson arrested me for a crime I didn't commit, and I think he had me beaten up, too."

"Then we need to go to the police and tell them what he did!"

"Don't. I want to stay here with you. I'm not ready to face the world just yet."

I nod.

"The beating took me back to a bad place. I couldn't pull myself out of it. My body and soul were stuck in the past, but my heart was stuck with you, and that's what kept me going. You're the reason I'm still alive."

I wish I could tell him what he wants to hear. I wish I could say I love him, that I trust him. But then I'd be lying. So, I tell him as much truth as I can.

"Rocco, before you came along, I was surviving on a day-to-day basis. I lived for luxuries and people-pleasing. I never acted out; I was always the responsible one, and a lot was expected of me. I never let myself be selfish. Not once did I feel how I feel with you."

"And how do you feel?" he asks cautiously, like he's afraid of my answer.

"Like you put life back into me. You've taught me to be myself fearlessly. You've shown me how to have fun regardless of the repercussions. With you, I feel happy, loved, understood, and listened to; all emotions that were foreign to me before. I've also felt angry and hurt because I can't break down my wall to trust you. As much as I try to, I don't hate you anymore."

Rocco sits up, wincing from the pain, and his lips lightly brush my cheek. "I know I said I hated you, too, but I could never hate you, Rosie. Never."

I lean my cheek into his palm and look into his eyes. I could stare into them forever.

"Thank you."

"For what?"

"For helping me get my humanity back."

"You're welcome. Now, can we go to the police?"

"No. I appreciate your concern. I do. But I think something deeper is going on with Officer Coleson. He has a vendetta against me, and I will find out why, without going to his boss first."

"Okay, if that's what you want."

"It is." He looks at his phone. "Is it ten already?"

I laugh. "Yeah, the day flew by."

"Shit. I'm sorry. I didn't mean to keep you so long. You didn't have to stay."

"I wanted to," I reassure him, even though I can't stay much longer. "I have somewhere to be tonight. Are you okay if I head out? I can come to your house in the morning if you need me."

"Hot date?" I can tell he's joking, but based on his unwavering stare, he's also dying to know if I'm meeting up with a guy.

"Not exactly, no. I'm glad you're back, Rocco. I may be the only reason you live, but you're the only reason I know how to live."

CHAPTER 18

Rocco

If Rosie thinks I won't follow her, she's sorely mistaken. I may have lost my humanity for a moment, but I'm back. She wouldn't tell me where she was going, which bothers me. What if something happens to her and I don't know where she is? I'd get no sleep tonight, so shortly after she leaves, I follow.

Lo and behold, she pulls into *La Citta del Peccato*. I don't know why she wouldn't tell me she was going to the club. It's like my second home. I would have gone with her in a heartbeat if she had asked. The only reason I could see her withholding the information was if she had a date, and she didn't exactly deny it when I brought that scenario up.

I know I shouldn't go inside. I shouldn't care about what she's doing or who she's with, but I do. It's wrong of me to spy on Rosie, but to be fair, she's done it to me.

I see the back of her head as she walks stealthily through the crowd, ignoring people who try to hit on her or start a conversation. Like a shadow amid the chaos, she moves directly toward the hallway in the back and opens the locked door to the basement with a key I didn't know she had. Before the door shuts, I quietly stop it with my hand. I contemplate doing the right thing by turning around and leaving, but then I remember who I am. Rocco Accardi doesn't do the right thing; he does what he wants. Right now, I want to know what the hell Rosanna is doing in the off-limits basement of the club.

Sitting on the back of my heels, I remain at the top of the stairs where the wall hides me. Rosie's boots shuffle across the floor. "Keep him waiting. I need a second to change."

"Take your time. I could keep him here for days if I wanted to."

Angelina is here? What the hell are they doing with a guy? I swear, if this is some kind of threesome, I will throw them both over my shoulder. I'm not sharing Rosie, and I'm not letting Angelina break Nicolai's heart. He may not agree, but we've become close friends lately.

"I have an early nail appointment tomorrow, so we can't keep him late. My cuticles are horrendous."

"Gia, don't be so dramatic. You got them done last week," Angelina states.

"Yeah, and one of them chipped! You know I can't stand when one is different from the others."

I hear a door open in the distance, and I lean down to peek over the wall. I don't even know where to look. The first thing I see is Rosie. She's changed into black cargo pants, a tank, and her typical combat boots. And her short, inky hair is pulled back into a messy ponytail. She looks badass and sexier than ever. But I don't get the chance to stare at her for long because the next thing I see is a man tied to a pole in the basement with tape over his mouth. What in the actual fuck is going on?

Gia and Angelina are also decked out in black, with their hair tied. All three girls match, and if I weren't so confused, I'd think it's cool as hell. Gia leans against a table, filing her nails as if there isn't a man tied to the ground beside her. Angelina circles the pole, gliding her finger across a knife like she's testing the sharpness. And Rosie is standing with her arms crossed, watching the victim like a hawk.

"Rosanna, open the file and tell this fucker why he's here," Angelina demands.

My rose drops a stack of photos on the ground next to the man, but I'm too far away to see them.

"In these pictures are five different girls, all under the age of eleven years old. Where are their clothes? Why do they look so scared? You took these pictures, didn't you?"

I hear the sound of tape ripping flesh. "How did you get these?" the man questions.

"I'm the one asking questions, not you," Rosie reprimands. "Answer me or suffer the consequences."

"Yeah, okay, like a bunch of girls are going to scare me."

Angelina smiles deviously and walks up to the victim.

"First, we're going to break you down mentally piece by piece until you're sitting in tears, at the lowest point of your life. Second, you're gonna be in so much pain that you'll wish for death to do you a favor and visit early. Third, and last, you're going to regret every single picture you took." There is no way those words just came out of Rosie's mouth. I'm not scared, but I sure as hell am surprised. I've never heard her talk like that.

Rosanna leans down and whispers in his ear. I can't hear her, but based on the man's shaking, it's not a comforting conversation. He starts begging for forgiveness and for God to save him. Tears run down his face, and my rose smiles like she's proud of making him break.

When she backs away, Angelina steps in. "Five girls deserve five screams from you."

She steps on his leg and breaks it. One scream. Next, she pulls his finger back, cracking the knuckle. Two screams. She continues physically breaking him apart for what feels like forever. Watching Angelina torture someone has truly made me frightened of her; she has some creative methods of pain. Remind me never to get on her bad side.

The man begs for mercy. "Please let me go. Or kill me."

"Alright, we're feeling kind today. Tell us the name of your accomplice, and we will end all of this," Angelina bargains.

"I don't have one."

"Do you think we're stupid?"

"No, no! Of course not."

"Then give us a name. We know you had one. If you lie, I promise to find you in Hell and finish what we started."

"Matteo Agosti. He will be attending the masquerade ball tomorrow night. It's invite-only, high-class, and nearly impossible to get on the list."

Rosanna scoffs, "I'm a Mariano. I can get us on the list."

"Now will you let me go?" the blubbering man asks with a hint of hope in his voice.

My legs start aching from the uncomfortable position, and I try to stand, making the step creak.

"Is someone there?" Angelina calls.

Shit. Some spy you are, Rocco.

"We know you're there. Come down, or we will chase you and we will find you."

I sigh and accept defeat.

"Help me!"

When I make it down the stairs, there's a gun pointed at my head.

"Dude, chill!" I yell because I don't want to die today. Nicolai was so quiet in the corner, I didn't even know he was there.

He lowers the gun. "Rocco?"

"Oh my God. Did you follow me?" Rosie does not sound happy.

"No. You don't get to ask the questions first. Why are you holding a man captive down here?"

She looks at the other girls as if she's unsure how to answer me.

Angelina sighs, rolling her eyes. "Tell him."

"Tell me what?"

"We're Whispers of Vice and Virtue," Rosie confesses.

What?

No.

No, that's impossible.

"You can't be. I've heard rumors, and all of them assume it's guys."

"Yeah, we try to do a good job at making people think that," Angelina deadpans.

"All of those victims in the news, were you three?"

They all nod, and I think I'm in shock. "Nicolai, you knew?"

"Angelina can't keep secrets from me. Plus, I'm the one who trained her," he declares proudly.

"Rosie? Why didn't you tell me?"

"You want the truth?"

"Please."

"I don't trust you."

"That's fair," I sigh, defeated.

"Call the police!" the man yells. I forgot about him.

"You sold child pornography? I'm not going to help you." I look at the girls, but they don't move. "Well, what are you waiting for? Don't stop on my account."

Angelina pulls a knife from her belt. "You're sure you want to see this? It's not pretty."

"Oh, for fuck's sake. Quit acting like I can't handle a little blood. I'm in the mafia. I'm your partner. You know I want to see it."

With my enthusiastic permission, she doesn't hesitate to slit his throat, spraying blood in an arch. Now the change of clothes makes sense. The girls walk up to his body, and I already know what they're about to do. I've seen the images in the news.

Across his forehead, in pink lipstick, Gia writes the word "Child." On his cheek, Rosie writes "Porn" in black, and lastly, Angelina writes "Ur next" on his chin in red.

"What do you do with his remains?"

"We take a picture and send it to the press anonymously, so it goes on the news. Then Nicolai takes care of the body, and Gia cleans up the crime scene," Rosie explains.

"You're sure they can't trace the murders to you?" I ask, worried that the girls will get into trouble. I'm sure I'd be able to get them out of jail. But there are no guarantees.

"Trust me, this basement will be more spotless than before we started. No spec of blood, DNA, or evidence is left behind," Gia states confidently. From what I've heard, she's extremely OCD, so I believe it.

"I'm impressed with all of you, but especially Rosie. I don't know how you kept this a secret from me for so long."

"I can keep a secret." She winks, subtly referring to us. No one else knows we crossed the line of being "just friends." We're way more than that.

Rosie saunters up to me and whispers in my ear, "Do you want to go to the masquerade ball tomorrow night with me?"

"Are you asking me on a date?" I inquire, trying my best not to smile like a kid who just got asked to prom.

"One date. One night of fun. Just because we're going together doesn't mean we're boyfriend and girlfriend."

"Of course, I'll be your date, sweetheart."

I'm going to make it a night she remembers forever.

CHAPTER 19

Rosanna

"That's it, I'm not going."

Angelina, Gia, and I have been walking around town for hours looking for dresses and masks to wear to the ball. Angelina found a stunning long red number with spaghetti straps and matching gloves, and Gia had a hard time choosing because she loved all of them. Eventually, we convinced her to get the strapless glittery gold gown with a large tulle skirt. Both were perfect, and my friends looked beautiful. Meanwhile, I tried on at least ten dresses, but none seemed like me. They're either too poofy, bland, too sparkly, or uncomfortable. I can't find the one that's just right, and we've been at it all day long. We need to leave and get ready for the ball soon, but the girls insist on finding me a dress.

"Let me text Rocco an update."

Me: Hey. I'm running late. I'm having trouble finding a dress for the ball. If we can't find one in the next half hour, I'm gonna have to cancel.

Rocco: Absolutely not, sweetheart. I'll take care of it.

Me: Um, no. No offense, but how do I know you have good taste?

Rocco: I know you don't trust me, but please have confidence in this one thing. Give me one hour. In the meantime, go get your nails done or whatever it is you girls do for these types of things.

Me: Thank you.

Rocco: You're welcome. I'll see you soon.

"Okay, so Rocco claims he will find me a dress I love, so you guys are off the hook," I inform the girls.

"This sounds like it's getting serious," Angelina observes.

"It's not. It's just a date. I didn't want to go alone." I convince myself of the words coming out of my mouth, even though they aren't true.

"Whatever you say," Gia pretends to agree. "Look, there's a nail salon! Perfect timing."

We each get a manicure and pedicure. Angelina gets red, Gia gets rose gold, and I get black. I don't know what color my dress will be, but black goes with everything, right?

Once our nails are dry, we drive to my house for hair and makeup. My family has a team for these types of events, so getting someone who will do a good job was easy.

"Cece!" Angelina and Gia both run up to my mother and hug her. The girls know she's hard on me, but she's never spoken that way toward them. She praises my friends like they're angels sent from heaven.

"I missed you girls. Rosanna doesn't bring you around enough, but you're always welcome," my mother gushes.

"Come. The makeup and hair team is set up in the loft. They're all ready for you girls."

"Thank you, Cece. It lifts a lot of stress off my shoulders to have someone else take care of my hair. My curls don't last an hour when I do them," Angelina says.

"You have beautiful, long blonde hair. Rosanna could've gotten hers this long if she didn't cut it," my mother complains, sending me a look of disappointment.

The second we step foot in the loft, we are immediately ushered into tall, foldable chairs. My hair and makeup artist is a very kind woman in her early thirties. Throughout the session, she compliments my facial features often and gushes over my hair, making me feel pretty and confident. When she finishes with my makeup, my eyes are smoky and dark, and my lips are lightly tinted red. I look amazing.

"What do you think?"

"Are you kidding? I love it!" I exclaim.

"Perfect! Now, let's get started on your hair."

The bell rings, so I get up to answer the door and come face-to-face with Rocco, who stares at me in awe.

"Whoa."

"Save your 'whoa' for later. My hair isn't even done yet, and I don't have a dress."

"You do now." He hands me a garment bag.

"Thank you again for doing this."

"Who is it?" my mother yells right before she walks around the corner.

"Oh boy," I mutter under my breath. "Mom, this is Rocco. My date to the ball."

As soon as my father hears "date," he comes running down the hall.

"It's a pleasure to meet you both," Rocco says, shaking my father's hand.

"Nice to meet you. I'm Raffaele. This is my wife, Cecelia. What was your name again?"

"Rocco Accardi, sir."

My mom goes pale. We're Marianos, meaning we know everyone in this town. I do not doubt that they've heard of Rocco's criminal record. But that doesn't mean people forget about his past. He has a reputation, and it's not a pretty one.

"You need to leave."

"Cecelia!" My father only ever uses her full name when he's angry with her.

"I know exactly who you are. I do not want you associated with my daughter."

"Respectfully, ma'am, I am taking Rosie to the ball whether you like it or not," Rocco states.

"Excuse me?" No one has ever talked to my mother that way. Typically, people agree with her and go along with whatever she says. Honestly, it's refreshing to have someone finally stand up to her.

"I apologize. I would have loved to make a good first impression, but that's quite literally impossible when you tell me the one thing I won't agree with."

"Get out," my mother demands.

"Pick me up in an hour?!" I shout before she shuts the door in his face.

"You are not to see that boy. He's bad news, Rosanna."

"I can make my own decisions, thank you."

Ignoring my Mom's spluttering protests, I hang the garment bag up and then walk back into the loft so my stylist can work on my hair. While she's curling my short strands, my phone dings.

Rocco: That went well.

Me: Ignore her. She'll get over it.

Rocco: I'll win her over one day.

Me: Good luck with that.

Rocco: I can't wait to see you in that dress. Be back in less than an hour.

"All done!"

I look up from the phone and stare at my reflection in the mirror. My hair is a curly half-updo, and it's as stunning as my makeup.

I hug my stylist. "I feel so beautiful. Thank you so much."

"Go get dressed, girl!"

I bolt up the stairs to change into the gown that Rocco got me. I'm excited to see it, but also very nervous. What if it's ugly? What if it won't fit? What if he doesn't know me at all?

I unzip the bag, and all of my worries fly out the door. I don't know where he could have possibly found a dress like this, but it is gorgeous. The bodice is a lacy corset with long, off-shoulder sleeves. And the silk slit skirt naturally flows to the floor; neither too tight nor too poofy. It's surprisingly comfortable, and it flatters my curves.

If I could have commissioned a gown for myself, it would be this masterpiece.

When I go to hand the garment bag in my closet, I feel the slightest bit of weight at the bottom. Curious, I pull out a lacy black mask attached to a rose and a note.

To my sweet rose,

Please let me spoil you more often. I had way too much fun shopping for you. -R

My cheeks go warm, and I tuck the rose into the back of my hair. It's just what I need to tie the look together. I place the mask over my eyes, tie it behind my head, and look in the mirror one last time. Not once in my entire life have I felt so beautiful.

"Rosanna! Are you coming?" Angelina yells. The girls must be ready.

"Coming!"

I round the corner and look down at where everyone is waiting. Rocco's back is turned away from me as he gets a picture with Nicolai. When he hears my heeled combat boots on the staircase, he spins around. I swear he stops breathing. He doesn't even blink, and I can't seem to look away from him either.

My date is dashing in a black suit with a dark grey button-up, and the ensemble is finished with a silver, metallic mask. He got a haircut, too. The top is still a mess of wavy locks, but the sides are shaved down. It sharpens his facial features and makes him look even sexier.

"Rosanna Mariano, you are exquisite," Rocco murmurs as his lips kiss the top of my palm.

I feel my cheeks go warm. "Thank you. This dress is perfect, and you look very handsome."

He gasps. "Was that a compliment?"

"The one and only."

Rocco puts a hand on my bare lower back to guide me out the door. "C'mon, we have a date to go on, and I don't plan on wasting a second of it."

CHAPTER 20

Rocco

Rumor has it this ball is for a cancer charity, but I guarantee half of the people in this room donate to hide their true colors. I already recognize a few faces that my father has worked with in the past. Luckily, though, none of them can identify me with a mask on. I'd rather not waste my night with Rosie on meaningless conversations with people undeserving of my time.

I look over at my date, and her head is craned toward the ceiling. She looks speechless. I know exactly how she feels. Rosanna is always a sight for sore eyes, but tonight, there are no words that do justice to how she looks.

Beautiful is the word I'd use when she wakes up in the morning with a messy bob and drowsy eyes.

Pretty is far too dull a word for a girl like her.

Ethereal is when she is fearless, strong, and ruthless.

Exquisite is how my rose looks tonight.

She spins slowly, and I don't think she has blinked. The ballroom looks like a scene out of a movie. The high-vaulted ceilings are painted with a vintage design that makes the place feel like old money. Tall, white pillars sit in the corners of the room, and the marble floors are so shiny that I can see my reflection. A large chandelier illuminates the space in an otherworldly glow as live classical music plays in the distance. It's peaceful and, for once, my mind has stopped running.

I don't think about the people around me, why we're here, or my problems outside of this room. All I think about is Rosie. The way her eyes sparkle as she watches couples waltz around. Or the way she closes her eyes and hums to the classical tune as if she's heard it before and it's her favorite melody. I can't possibly think about anything else when she looks the way she does tonight. I always figured the saying "love at first sight" was an exaggeration. A myth, or an outright lie. But when I saw Rosie walk down those stairs, I knew exactly what that saying meant. At that moment, I knew I loved Rosanna Mariano.

"Are you gonna ask me to dance or shall I find another eligible bachelor?" Rosie asks.

"Like hell, you're dancing with another man." I bow and offer my hand. "May I have this dance?"

She places her palm in mine. "I thought you'd never ask."

I don't know how to waltz or dance like everyone else, but Rosie makes it look effortless. I move where she moves, and hope I'm not making a fool of myself. At least I haven't stepped on her toes.

"Think you can manage a twirl?" she whispers with a hint of mocking in her tone.

"Absolutely." *Not.*

She sidesteps, extends her arm, and spins back into my body. I catch her with ease. That wasn't so hard.

She doesn't remove herself from my arms. Our faces are so close. Her chest barely moves as if she is holding her breath, and her eyes stare at my mouth with clear desperation. The song ends right as I start to lean forward.

"Welcome, everyone! I want to thank you for showing up at the National Foundation of Cancer Research charity event. We've already had many generous donations, and I am so grateful for every penny. With that being said, I'd like to begin the raffle! Whoever bids the highest will win a two-week-long trip to my beach house in Hawaii!" a man, who I'm assuming is the event's host, shouts over the microphone. "Bid starts at five hundred, do I have eight?"

Someone in the distance raises their hand. "One thousand!"

An older woman next to me throws her hand in the air. "Two thousand!"

The next few minutes are a rush of shouts, hands in the air, and gasps of shock. The last offer was nine thousand, and no one has spoken since.

"Going once, twice, SOLD to the gentlemen in the blue!" The host is beaming over the raffle results. "Please come receive the keys, and we would love to get a picture with you. Your donation is the most generous we have received in years! What is your name, sir?"

"Matteo Agosti."

Rosie sucks in a sharp breath. That's the man they needed to find tonight, and he just made the girls' job a lot easier. "That's him."

"I know. What's your plan?"

"Follow me." She walks away, and I obey, placing my palm on her lower back so people know better than to ask her to dance or steal her from me. We leave the ballroom, and I'm certain she has no idea where she's going. She peeks into a bathroom, a few guest rooms, and a loft area.

"Taking a tour, sweetheart?"

"We need a place to take him where we won't be found or heard."

I look around and spot a staircase. "What about down there?"

Immediately, she rushes down the stairs without hesitation. "It's perfect," I hear her say as I follow. "It's far down, and the walls are thick enough that no one will hear. There's even a solid door before the wine cellar. You and Nico need to guard it. Can you do that?"

"Of course, we can. I'll let him know. When?"

"I'm going to flirt with Matteo and lure him here. I will send you a signal right before I bring him down the stairs."

"Why do you have to be the one to flirt? Why not Angelina or Ginevra? No, don't answer that. Nicolai would break Matteo's neck if he touched her. But what about Ginevra?"

"Gia is the one who preps the murder, making sure we have what we need to get away with this. She can't be out there flirting because I need her down here preparing for a bloodbath," Rosie explains.

"Fine. But if his lips get anywhere near yours, I will throw you over my shoulder without hesitation. He's not allowed to kiss you, nor you him. Understood?"

I haven't had a chance to kiss her tonight, so no chance in hell is he going to get the privilege.

"Okay, Mr. Dramatic. C'mon, I don't have all night, and who knows how long Matteo will stay." She returns to the ballroom, and I remain in a corner where I will have a perfect view of them together.

Rosie walks up to him with a fake smile. I know what her real smile looks like. His gaze zones in on her exposed leg slit and then her cleavage, and it makes me want to gouge his eyeballs out. She touches his bicep and giggles at something he said. He then takes her hand, leading her into a waltz, and she steps on his foot. I know for a fact she can dance effortlessly. My rose is probably acting stupid, so he thinks less of her and is more trusting. When she throws her head back and laughs, his lips make contact with her neck, and the glass in my hand shatters.

"Fuck."

A few pieces cut my hand, but nothing so brutal that it would need stitches. I cover it up with a napkin to soak up the dripping blood.

I look up and see Rosie staring right at me as Matteo faces the other way. She winks, and I'm gonna take a lucky guess that it's my signal. I text Nico to let him know it's time, as Rosie takes Matteo's hand and leads him off the dance floor. I follow far enough behind them that he won't see me, but I hasten my steps when he gets through the wine cellar door. Then I barge in.

He tries to lean in for a kiss, but before he can, I shove his shoulder, and my fist makes contact with his nose.

"Damnit, Rocco, you're supposed to stay outside! Let me handle him." Rosie is not happy with me.

"I said he couldn't kiss you. I meant it."

"Is this your boyfriend or something?"

Matteo asks.

I wink at Rosie. "Something like that."

"Hey, guys!" Ginevra comes out from

around a corner, jump scaring the shit out of me.

"Who the fuck is she?" I can tell Matteo's

starting to lose patience.

"I don't feel like making up excuses or

manhandling him. Rocco, could you do me a favor

and tie him down?" Rosie requests with a pout.

Fuck. I will do anything for this girl. She has me

whipped. "Anything for you, sweetheart."

"I'm sorry. What? I'm getting out of here.

I'm not into any kinky shit with you three." Matteo

goes to leave, but I step in front of him, blocking

the door. My body doesn't move an inch when he

tries to shove me out of the way. Wrapping a hand around his throat, I throw him against a wall, making him choke, but I don't let up.

His lips touched my girl. His tongue tasted what's mine. He eye fucked what belongs to me. *I'm going to have so much fun with this one.*

"Rocco, you're going to kill him," a faint voice says.

My captive claws at my hand, probably scratching it and drawing blood. I don't care. I welcome the pain.

"Let go."

The fear in his irises is undeniable.

"Rocco"

His face turns a shade of purple.

"Rocco!"

I'm yanked off of him, and I blink, taking in my surroundings. I completely lost control. Nicolai is standing next to me. He must have been the one to pull me away.

"Shit, sorry. I must have lost control."

"For once, I relate to you. If that was Angel, I would have killed him much faster than you almost did," Nicolai remarks.

"Okay, so Rosanna is no longer allowed to be the distraction. Next time, I'll find a way to do it," Ginevra states.

Rosanna walks up to me and shakes her head, but based on her grin, she's not actually upset. "The drama."

I lean in close to her ear so her friends can't hear and whisper, "You're mine. Not his. Not

Aimone's. Not Leonardo's. I'm done sharing. Next time you're the distraction, I will kill the man before you girls can even get to him."

CHAPTER 21

Rosanna

Rocco and Nicolai stand outside the door while we get started. I had to kick my date out after he almost killed our victim. After Matteo was secured, the girls and I changed into our "uniforms", putting our dresses in a spot where they can't get dirty. Gia brought the clothes, weapons, a tarp, trash bags, cleaning supplies, and much more. I have no clue how she snuck all of that in here without getting caught.

"HELP!"

"Aw, you poor thing. Do you think anyone can hear you down here? These walls are made of stone," I taunt.

"Why are you doing this to me?"

"I'm getting tired of answering that question. I want to have a little fun this time. You're gonna guess why you're here, and each time you're wrong, my friend Angelina will inflict pain however she sees fit. So, why are you here, Matteo?"

"Look, if I slept with one of you and I don't remember, I apologize, I must have blacked out—"

Zap. Angelina tases him.

His body spasms, but he can handle much more pain than that. He's gonna have to.

"None of us would ever sleep with you. When your tongue met my neck in that ballroom, I had to swallow back puke." Unfortunately, that's not a lie. "Let's try this again. Why are you here?"

"Did someone hire you to torture me? If so, I don't see why they'd hire a bunch of girls."

Zap. Zap. Zap.

"Oh, I'm sorry, would you rather we be younger?"

"Excuse me?" He looks confused but also terrified.

"You're taking up too much of my time. I have a date to get back to, so I'm gonna tell you why you're here, and then Angelina is going to kill you… This is the part where you ask me why you're here."

"Why am I here?" he whimpers, scared.

"You're here because your partner was a rat."

"Was?"

"He told us all about you. I was kind of disappointed with how easily he caved and started mouthing off. We know about the five girls you photographed."

"No, no, you got it all wrong. He did that! I had nothing to do with it," Matteo pleads. Lies. We got proof that he was involved after we killed his partner.

"I'm not interested in your lies. Angelina, I'm done here." I'd usually like to spend more time torturing our victim, but I want to enjoy my night with Rocco. Not away from him.

"Why don't we put all this wine to good use? After all, it's wasting away in this cellar. Gia?" Angelina inquires, asking for permission.

"Ugh, fine, but at least save me a bottle," Gia grumbles as she scrolls on her phone.

"Open wide," Angelina instructs Matteo. When his lips remain in a firm line, she pries his mouth open and starts pouring wine. He coughs and chokes on the liquid. Once the first bottle runs out, the second starts pouring down his gullet, giving him no time to breathe or swallow. By the time she gets to the fifth bottle, he's dead.

CHAPTER 22

Rocco

I'm not proud to admit that when Rosie opens the cellar door— earlier than I anticipated, might I add— Nicolai and I are playing Rock, Paper, Scissors. It took a lot to convince him to indulge me, mainly a promise to shut up about it, and he beat me multiple times. It was getting boring, so don't blame me for thinking of something to do.

"Rock, paper, scissors? How old are you two?" Angelina questions as Rosanna laughs at us.

"We're bonding!"

"Shut the fuck up before I beat your ass."

Nicolai's love language is violence. *He loves me.*

I grab Rosie's hand and lead her back upstairs. When she tries to go back to the ballroom, I don't let go and keep walking.

"Where are we going?"

"I'm done being patient."

"Okay, then go home. I can find a ride," she says with displeasure.

That's not what I meant. "No. I'm done being patient with you. I need you, Rosie."

"You want me? Then you'll have to catch me."

What? "You're wearing combat boots with heels, Rosanna. You can't run from me."

She leans down, giving me a full view of her cleavage, as she attempts to remove her shoes.

When she fumbles with the clasp, I drop to one knee.

We make eye contact as my hand glides down from her exposed thigh all the way down to her ankle. Her body shivers, and it lights up my insides to know I have such an effect on her. I unzip and remove her boot, then move onto the other side before handing them to her.

"Such a gentleman."

"Occasionally." *For her and only her.*

I lean in so my lips touch her ear. I love doing that, and based on her body's instant reaction, she does, too. "Run."

Rosie bolts down the hall. When she gets to the end, she glances back and giggles before taking off down another corner.

After a few seconds' head start, I give chase.

This house is a mansion. A maze. I turn left where she did, but I am met with more doorways and halls. It's too quiet.

"Rosie, if you're hiding, I will find you. You're better off running," I warn.

I hid from my father a lot when I was a kid, so I know all the best spots, even if this isn't the same house.

I walk through the bathroom, checking the shower and behind the door, and search the adjoining bedroom next. She's not under the bed, in the closet, behind the door, or in the curtains. I open the hallway storage closet, expecting her to be there, but I have no luck. Where is she? Sneaky little thing. I catch her head poking out of another guest room before she bolts, and I run after her. I'm losing patience, so I'm not going to go easy on her.

Rosie tries to shut the kitchen doors behind her, but my hand stops them from closing. I don't know what the host does for a living, but the fact that he has an extra kitchen for guests tells me enough.

Rosie slowly backs up as I stalk forward, shutting and locking the double doors behind me. They're the only way out, and I'm not letting her pass.

"I win. Now, sit your pretty ass on that counter and let me claim my prize."

She lifts herself onto the countertop and crosses her legs, exposing more skin.

I grab her thighs, yanking them apart and opening her wide. But before I can taste what's mine, Rosie puts her hand on my head.

"Say please."

I have never pleaded for anything after I was made to beg for mercy my whole childhood. Since I became an adult, I have refused to humble myself like that in front of any woman or man. Hell, I would let someone torture me before asking for death or mercy.

For Rosie, though? I'll push past all of my vulnerabilities and do as she orders without hesitation. "Please, sweetheart."

She drops her hand, permitting me to continue. I lick, suck, and bite, doing all of the things that drive her mad. Every time she gets close to the edge, I slow down, refusing her orgasm. Now she knows how impatient I felt watching her dance with someone else. When she's seconds away from her release again, I rise and walk over to the refrigerator.

"What the hell are you doing? You can't just stop and walk away!"

"Calm down, sweetheart. I'm curious." The fridge is fully stocked. The host probably has people who grocery shop for him, and I bet he wastes all this food every week. Might as well put some of it to good use, right?

So many options.

Whipped cream.

Fudge.

Strawberries.

Ice cream…

I grab two ice cubes and pop them in my mouth. They immediately start melting, and damn it's cold.

Rosanna watches me with eyes full of awe, lust, and a hint of curiosity.

I get on one knee, open my mouth, and glide an ice cube from her thigh to her center. It leaves a path of cold water, and she shivers. When the ice makes contact with her cunt, she jolts up from the countertop. Rosie may be jumpy, but her moan is a dead giveaway that she enjoys it.

I hold her legs down with both my hands so she can't move, and within seconds, she chants my name as I ravish her. I spit out the remaining ice, pull out my hard-on, and thrust into her without warning. Instead of her usual warmth, a slight chill embraces me tightly.

"Say you need me," I groan.

I halt any movement.

"I need you."

Thrust.

"Tell me you won't let anyone else touch you."

Halt.

"Only you can touch me."

Thrust.

"Remind me that you're mine."

Halt.

Instead of words, she kisses me slowly, sensually, and passionately. "Do you want to know a secret?"

"Always."

"You were my first kiss. My first everything," she divulges as if she didn't just drop a bomb on me.

"Rosanna, if you're lying to me right now —"

"I'm not. I was never careless in high school. I didn't have the time, and I was too scared because of my family name. Maybe if I met someone worth it, I would have, but I never once felt that any guy was deserving of me. Not until you."

"Why didn't you tell me sooner? I would have been gentle during your first time. Oh, God, did I hurt you? I'm so sorry, sweet—"

She places a finger to my lips, stopping me from spiraling. "No, stop thinking like that. I didn't tell you because I didn't want you to treat me like some porcelain doll. You did nothing wrong."

I rest my forehead against hers and take a deep breath, trying hard not to get lost in my head. I feel like a total douchebag. That was her first time.

"Rocco, I wanted everything you gave me that night. Every single thing. I don't regret a second, and I wouldn't change any of it." She lifts her hips impatiently. "If you don't start moving inside of me right now, I will go back downstairs and find a stranger to finish the job."

I growl. I'm done sharing her, and Rosie knows it. She's using that to her advantage, but damn her, it's working. I start rocking my hips.

"So, you're saying no one else has kissed you? No one has been inside of you like this but me?"

"Well, you were my first kiss, yes, but I never said no one else has kissed me."

Halt.

"Give me a name," I demand.

"Roc—"

"Name, Rosanna." She knows I only use her full name when I'm not messing around.

"It was Leo."

Godfuckingdamnit. I hate that guy.

"You can't kill him," she cautions.

"Why not?"

"It was a kiss. He doesn't deserve to die for that."

I tilt my head down. "I beg to differ."

"Rocco, drop it and fuck me already."

I fuck her senseless until she's gone over the edge. Only after she's satisfied do I fill her up and leave my cum dripping down her leg.

"Don't you dare clean that up. You're wearing my cum all night."

I brush her wavy bob down with my fingers, wipe her under eyes free of smeared mascara, and straighten her mask. I drop to one knee again, lift her feet, and zip up her boots one by one. As soon as she's ready, I lead her into the ballroom.

Nicolai and Angelina are waltzing and laughing in the middle of the crowd. I figured they would have left after the girls finished their business, but it seems my partner convinced her

ornery man to stay.

"One more dance." I offer my hand, and

Rosie takes it.

She lays her head on my shoulder as we

slowly dance to a classical tune. Halfway through

the song, she lifts her head, and her eyes are dead

set on a man with a full-face black mask standing in

a corner.

"Do you know him?"

"No. Not that I know of, but he's been

watching us for this whole song."

He's making Rosie uncomfortable, and I'm not

okay with that. I try to approach him, but before I

can, I run right into the body of Leonardo Capponi.

"I am so sorry, man," he apologizes.

Alexandra Bianchi walks out from behind him and puts a hand on his back, staking her claim. She eyes Rosanna up and down and makes a face of disgust. "Told you she was a slut. She's already found a new man. Wonder who her next one will be."

I can't punch a girl. So, I punch Leonardo. For the comment his date made, for kissing my girl, and for breaking her heart.

Nicolai and Angelina rush over to us as Rosie slaps Alex across the face. I am so proud of her. Leonardo tries to throw a punch at me, but I duck before his fist makes contact. The man is way too predictable.

I should have taken one for the team, though, because I did not see Angelina right behind me, and she wasn't paying attention as the fucker's fist made contact with her face. Now, her nose is dripping blood. Luckily, her dress is red.

"Oh, you are seriously going to regret that," Nicolai growls.

Leonardo freaks out. "It was an accident! I would never hit a girl. Rocco moved!"

"I don't give a shit how it happened. All I care about is that my girl is bleeding."

This is about to get bad.

Nicolai pulls out a gun from his suit jacket and points it at Leonardo's forehead.

The man's face pales, and he puts his hands up in the air. "Whoa, whoa, whoa. Calm down. I swear I didn't mean to. I'm so sorry. Please don't kill me."

At this point, the classical music has stopped, and everyone is staring or backing away from the scene.

And I hear police sirens getting closer outside. Someone must have called the cops. Wow, these people don't know how to party, do they? Snitches.

"We need to go. Let him go," I tell Nico.

He gestures at Angelina. "Look at her!"

"I know, man, I get it. But there are too many witnesses. You'd go to jail."

Nico stares at Leonardo's face and lowers the gun. "If you ever touch her again, accident or not, you will be begging for my mercy."

I see red and blue, and Officer Coleson walks through the front door.

"Run."

CHAPTER 23

Rosanna

My legs move faster than they ever have as we run from the cops. Rocco is behind me. I'm sure he can go much quicker, but I don't think he wants to take the chance of losing me. Nicolai and Angelina are ahead of us, but she's struggling to keep up because of her heels. So, her husband throws her over his shoulder and books it.

"Aw, do you want me to carry you, sweetheart?" Rocco shouts.

"Hell no. I can take care of myself."

"Atta girl."

Nico and Angelina yell at us to get in the car, and Officer Coleson bursts through the back door just as we peel out of the parking lot. I close my eyes, rest my head against the seat, and take deep breaths. It's a pain in the ass to run in boots with heels.

Nicolai pulls up to my house first. "Say goodnight, you two. There's no hiding that something is going on, so don't waste your time denying it." I guess we haven't been very good at hiding our "relationship."

Rocco leans over and lightly kisses my cheek. "Good night, sweetheart."

I smile at him before getting out and walking to the front door. "Al, what are you still doing up?"

"My job is to ensure you get home safely, Miss Mariano."

"Rosanna," I remind him.

He nods like he understands, yet he still calls me by my surname every time I see him.

I trudge upstairs to my bedroom, exhausted. I would love nothing more than to crash into bed, but I stop short at the rose sitting on my pillow. How does he keep doing this?

I pick up the rose and smell the floral scent embedded in its red petals.

To my sweet rose,

Thank you for being my date to the masquerade ball. I hope you knew you were the most beautiful girl in the room. Dream of me, as I will of you. -R

CHAPTER 24

Rocco

When I woke up this morning, I couldn't get my head on straight, and by midafternoon, I'm on my way to Rosie's house. All I can think about is our relationship. What are we? Does she trust me yet? Why can't I call her mine? In public. Not just privately.

After parking in front of her house, I shut off my bike and greet the butler, "Good afternoon, Al. I hope you got some sleep after waiting up so late."

"Afternoon, Mr. Accardi. I slept like a baby once Miss Mariano was safely inside."

"Thank you for looking out for her. Not just last night, but her entire childhood. She told me how long you've been with the family."

He bows. "The pleasure is all mine."

I try to hand him cash for sneaking a rose in last night with the note, but he shakes his head.

"No need. You make Miss Mariano happier than I have ever seen her. I don't need payment for assisting, given the smile you put on her face."

"Thank you, Al."

I'm sure he is not supposed to let me in the house, but he steps aside regardless.

I walk in and am met with silence. Luckily, Rosie's parents are out. I don't think they would have been happy to see me.

"Rosie?!"

"Hello?"

"It's Rocco. Where are you?"

"Coming!" She rushes down the stairs in leggings, a hoodie, and headphones dangling from her neck. I think she was about to leave on a run. "What are you doing here?"

"I couldn't sleep, eat breakfast, and my mind won't stop racing," I admit.

"Is something wrong? Oh my God, did something happen after you guys dropped me off? Angelina didn't call or text me."

"No, nothing like that."

"Then what?"

How do I lay my heart out for her despite the fear of getting it crushed? I don't want to lose Rosie, but I've become too selfish to only get bits and pieces. I've passed the point of wanting all of her. I'm in too deep. I need all of her or none because it hurts too much knowing she isn't truly mine.

"Forgive me," I plead.

"Rocco, I can't keep—"

"Please. Please forgive me. I can't do this anymore." My voice cracks. "It's tearing me apart. I know I said I would take all that you give me, but I'm suffering."

I'm ashamed of myself for not being stronger, for not being okay with all that she gives me. I wish more than anything that it's enough, but it's not. It never has been.

Her voice is barely a whisper. "I can't forgive you."

"Baby, please."

"Rocco, don't you get it? I can't!" she yells, and it feels as though my heart stops beating. "If I could forgive you, I would have already. I trust that you'd never hurt me. I trust you with my secrets. I trust your words and intentions."

Okay, so what is the problem?

"What I don't trust is you with my friends. I don't believe that you wouldn't put them in harm's way for your benefit. I worry that you'd do anything for money or a good deal. After all, isn't that why you hurt Angelina?"

And just like that, my heart breaks in half. Rather than making new memories with her, I will be remembering the old ones.

The future I hoped we would have can't exist in a world where she doesn't trust me.

I imagined a custom-made ring on her finger one day. I pictured a little boy with black curls running around in the backyard, while both of us fought for mommy's attention.

I would have given her the world if she had just let me.

Why wasn't I enough for her?

She continues, as if she hasn't said enough. "Even if I could forgive you, my parents would never approve of our relationship. We can't, and we won't work."

We won't work, or she's not willing to try?

"I'm going to let you go, and I would appreciate it if you let me walk away and never come looking for me. Because if you do, Rosanna, I will cave. I will miss you every second of every day, and I don't know if I'm strong enough to do this twice." I march out the front door before she can see the tears running down my cheek.

CHAPTER 25

Rosanna

I wake up sweating, my heart pounding, and my breathing erratic. I couldn't fall asleep last night, so I took melatonin, and it gave me a chilling nightmare. After Rocco left yesterday, I couldn't stop crying, and I'm not a crier. I said things in the heat of the moment that I regret, but they weren't entirely false either. My heart belongs to Rocco, but my head tells me not to trust his intentions when it comes to greed. He's always wanted more for himself, financially and in the mafia. Would he put himself before me and my friends? Would he sacrifice a good deal for safety and trust? Would he betray me? I don't know, and that is the problem.

Not only that, but my parents have already disapproved of Rocco. They want me to be with a man of high social status, a pristine reputation, and from a good family. Rocco has none of that. He's rich, but low on social status because of his known criminal record. He has no family, and his reputation is tarnished. Our relationship was doomed from the start.

I force my body out of bed and pull myself together for a morning run. It's the only thing that will clear my head. I brush through my shoulder-length hair and throw it in a small ponytail. Blue feels like the color of the day, so I choose my matching baby blue set for my run. And as soon as my shoes are on, I'm running out the door, in desperate need of fresh air and sunlight.

Except when I pass through the threshold, I'm met with pouring rain. It's still warm out, but the sun is nowhere to be seen. If I don't run this morning, I might do something I'll regret. Like calling Rocco, and I don't want to make this harder for him. Despite the dismal weather, I run on the sidewalk for ten minutes until I get to the park. I'm soaked from head to toe, and the running path is empty. It's not exactly the type of weather you take your kids out to.

Halfway through my run, I start to get cold. The skies are getting dark, and as much as I don't mind running in the rain, I do mind running in lightning. I turn around to head home and immediately run into a hard body. I must not have heard them behind me with my headphones on.

Usually, I'm aware of my surroundings, but today I was distracted. My mind was on something else, or rather someone else.

I pull my earbuds out. "I am so sorry. I am such a klutz. Are you alright?"

I stare up into a man's face. Late forties, black hair with grey streaks, and eyes that look familiar. Or at least, one of them.

"Excuse me?"

He doesn't answer. I try to go around him to run home, but as I pass, he grabs my arm. Tightly. I attempt to jerk out of his grip, but he doesn't let up. Now I'm starting to panic. I look around, but no one is here. The parking lot is empty, the park is deserted, and the running path is clear. I'm alone.

The man finally speaks. "You're going to come with me, and if you try to run away or cause a scene, I will shoot you in the back of the head. Do you understand?"

I shouldn't oblige. I know that whatever he has waiting for me is worse than this situation. But what choice do I have when he pulls out a loaded gun from his hoodie pocket?

"I understand."

CHAPTER 26

Rocco

It's early as hell, yet here I am playing poker and blowing through my money because I don't give a shit. A part of me hopes she'll show up. But that won't happen yet because she does her spy work at night. Nicolai met me at the club after I begged him relentlessly. He can tell I'm going through something, but he doesn't ask, and I'm grateful for that. I lost the next poker game, but honestly, even if I had won, I would feel nothing.

My phone buzzes in my pocket. I almost don't pull it out, but if it's Rosanna texting or calling, I want to know. I need to know if this is affecting her as much as it is me.

I drop my cards on the table and stare at the picture of Rosanna on the screen. I feel like I can't breathe.

Unknown number: Come alone, or she dies. I want one million wired to this account. You have an hour.

4459 Brera St

Link for transfer

"What's wrong?" Nicolai asks.

I show him the phone and start to pace, running my hands through my hair. "How the fuck am I going to get one million dollars? I'm rich, but not by that much. And even if I were, my bank would never let me transfer such a large sum at once."

Nicolai grabs both of my shoulders, stopping me in my tracks. "I can get you the money, but you're not going alone."

"Like hell, I'm not. Do you want her to die?!" I yell.

"Of course not. But no matter the circumstances, you can't go alone. The only reason Angelina survived is because Rosanna showed up for her, regardless of the threat. If you go alone, both of you are dead."

"Fine. But if Rosie dies because you get caught, I will never forgive you." I mean that with every fiber of my being.

"We're going to my house, then we will go get your girl."

"Why do we have to stop at your place?" I don't have the time or patience for that.

"Neither of us has enough weapons."

"We're taking my bike, then. It's faster."

Nico doesn't argue. We run out of the club, and I start my bike up. He gets on the back, promptly putting his hands on the rail behind the seat.

"Put your goddamn hands around me or you're gonna fall off," I tell him as his only warning before I take off.

We pull up to his house minutes later, and I leave the bike running while we go inside. In his basement, we grab as many weapons as we can hide on our bodies. I seize a pistol for myself and stuff it in my belt, and when I spot a stack of ninja stars next to the stairs, I decide to take a few of those, too, on a whim.

"You're going to drive your bike to the address, and I will follow. I won't be seen. Please, for the love of all things holy, do not shoot yourself on your way there with the gun in your pants," Nico instructs.

"Got it." I pull my helmet on and yell at Nicolai as he walks to his car. "Do not intrude unless you have to! If you show your face, they'll shoot her."

He nods, and I take off. In the rearview, I see him following, but not close enough for anyone to notice.

The address leads me to a nice neighborhood. White picket fences, two-story homes, and playgrounds in the backyard. It's not the type of place for crime.

I'm taken to a tan house with blue shutters. It looks fairly new, and the backyard is empty. The grass is freshly mowed, and the front door sign reads "Welcome." It's a picture-perfect house on the outside, but it's the inside that I want to see so desperately. Above the front door is a ring camera. I get a text.

Unknown number: Put all of your weapons under the plant to the right of the door. If I find one on you when you walk in, she's dead.

I pick up the artificial plant, revealing a hollow vase under it. The thing looked so real that I wouldn't have known it was fake. I place my gun and two ninja stars inside, right in front of the ring camera, so they can see. I have one more star, but I'm praying they won't find it.

I slowly step past the threshold. It's completely silent inside the house, and right after I shut the door, I feel a gun barrel pointed at my head from behind. I put my hands up.

After a quick pat down, they push my back, indicating that I should walk forward down the entrance hallway. The figure in a black hoodie behind me opens the door to the basement. They won't let me see their face, keeping their back to me, but based on their build and height, it's without a doubt a male.

When I get to the bottom of the basement stairs, I see her. Rosie's tied and gagged to a chair, and I take her face in my hands.

"You're going to be okay." My voice cracks. I'm trying my best to be strong for her, to convince her that we will both make it out alive, but she's scared. I can see it in the way her eyes fill with tears and fear. I slide the ninja star out of my sleeve without the guy noticing, and place it in her hand behind her back. She's going to get out of here, one way or another.

"Your money has been wired to the account you sent. Now let us go."

"Now, where's the fun in that?"

My hands stop moving. I stop breathing. I dare blink or move an inch. This isn't real. It's all just a nightmare. *It has to be.*

"Miss me, son?"

I ball my hands into fists, so he doesn't notice them shaking uncontrollably. I turn around, and the sight of him brings all my worst fears to life.

"How?" I whisper.

"You think I don't have a doctor on emergency dial? I thought I raised you to be smarter than that. You should have watched me die. Stupid boy," my father scolds.

The floor above us creaks. *Fucking Nicolai.*

"You didn't come alone. Did you?"

"I don't know who that is. I swear."

"You know, I might have let you two go if you listened. All of those years raising you, and you never once listened to my orders. Always rebelling, questioning my actions, or trying to be your mother's hero. Do you know I ran a paternity test? I thought, this boy can't possibly be mine. But then, it came back and showed that you've got my DNA. I was disappointed, just as I am now. You let me down. If you listened, I may have let her live."

He raises a gun, and the next few seconds go by in slow motion. Nicolai runs down the stairs, and Rosie's eyes meet mine like they're saying goodbye. I bolt across the room and hear a gunshot ring through the silence. I see my rose scream past the gag in her mouth as tears run down her cheeks. Then, there's a second gunshot.

My eyes never once leave Rosie's before I fall over, and my vision goes black.

CHAPTER 27

Rosanna

I scream so loud my throat burns. My hands were almost free of the ropes, but by the time I cut through them, it was too late. I yank the gag from my mouth and run to Rocco's unmoving form.

"ROCCO! Wake up. You have to wake up!" I shake his body so hard his head hits the concrete floor.

"Wake up. You have to wake up!"

"DO SOMETHING!" I shout at Nicolai.

I hold Rocco in my arms. Sobs wrack my body, and I can't stop them. "Please. I'm sorry that I never trusted you. I'm sorry I didn't give you a real chance. I'm sorry you're dead because of me." My apologies are barely understandable through my tears. "Most of all, I'm sorry I never told you I love you."

I rock him back and forth, begging him to come back to me.

The body in my arms moves. "I'm gonna need you to repeat all of that so I know I'm not dreaming."

"Rocco?"

"Alive and well, sweetheart. I apologize for the scare. I think I passed out in the heat of the moment."

"How? I watched you get shot. The bullet hit you. How are you alive?"

He sits up and unzips his leather jacket to reveal a bulletproof vest.

I punch him in the chest. Repeatedly.

"Ow!" He backs up.

"Why would you do that?! You got lucky. He could have hit anywhere else, and you could've been seriously injured!"

"You think I wouldn't take a bullet for you? That I wouldn't die for you? God, Rosanna, open your eyes. I would do anything for you."

"I love you," I confess before I can stop the words from pouring out of my mouth.

"I've always loved you," Rocco says right before I pull his leather jacket toward me and kiss him.

He pulls back. "Wait, where's my father?"

I stare at where his father lies on the ground, and Rocco walks over to the body. His fingers press against the inside of his father's wrists.

"This time I'm making sure."

"Didn't you say you killed him?"

"I thought I did. I left right after I stabbed him in the chest. I didn't stick around to wait for his heart to stop beating, though. He didn't deserve any more of my time or attention. I guess he found medical attention before he died."

"Is he dead this time?"

"Yeah. There's no pulse or heartbeat."

Nicolai walks up to Rocco and hugs him.

"I'm glad you're okay, man."

"Aw, you love me, too?"

"Yeah, yeah. Angelina would have been devastated if something had happened to Rosanna. I forgive you for all of it. If you'd take a bullet for Rosanna, I trust you with her safety and Angelina's. Consider us friends." Nico pats him on the shoulder, but he has no idea how happy this is making Rocco. All he's ever wanted is a true friend.

"Thank you. Now, if you don't mind, I'm going to take Rosie home."

"I'll call Ginevra, and we will get this taken care of."

"She loves a good mess," I state.

Rocco puts his arm around me and walks me out to his bike.

"So does this mean you're mine?" he asks.

"Rocco, I've always been yours."

EPILOGUE

Rocco

I convinced Rosanna to move in with me a few months later after that whole fiasco with my father. Rosanna's parents used to despise me for my reputation. They forbade me from seeing her and threatened me countless times. But after the shooting, Rosanna told them everything that went down, and they visited me in the hospital and gave me their blessing proudly. The life-threatening situation Rosie was in made them realize that her safety and happiness are far more important than money and reputation. They helped her move into my house a few months later, even though her father was emotional letting her go.

Somehow, not long after moving in, she convinced me to buy her a pit bull. Who am I kidding? I'd give her anything, no questions asked. Rosie named him Cannoli. As much as I wanted to protest, it was quite fitting. Our pit is hard on the outside, but a softie on the inside. He will attack anyone who seems alarming, but as soon as he sees me, Rosie, or even Nicolai, he's a baby.

When I walk through the front door, Canno jumps on me, and I pet behind his ears, telling him he's a good boy. He follows me to the living room, where I find the three girls having a sleepover. It's funny to me how one minute they're badass murderers and the next they're wearing face masks and painting nails.

I stand behind Rosie as she concentrates on painting her toe. When she looks up, I lean down to kiss her Spider-Man style, and whisper in her ear, "I expect those nails to be black, and I want them making marks all over me tonight." I kiss her cheek and walk away.

I grab the dying flowers from the table, throw them out, and replace the vase with new roses from Café Florian. I always keep flowers in the house; regardless of how busy my week is, I make time to stop for them. It makes my rose smile, and that's all I care about.

"C'mon, Canno, we got a hot date with Nicolai and poker. Let's leave Momma to her girls' night."

One day, shortly after we adopted Canno, I walked into the VIP lounge, and there was my dog sitting next to Nico, growling at other players.

I peek at Rosie, tell her I love her, and then walk out the door.

I love the life Rosie and I have built, and there is so much more in store for us. I will spend every day loving her and putting a smile on her face until death do us part.

Everyone has a story, and I saved the best for last.

Ginevra & Officer Coleson

* 9 7 9 8 2 1 8 6 7 7 3 3 6 *